finding peace

Bluebird
BAY

Other series by
Denise Grover Swank

Mystery:
Rose Gardner Mystery Series
Rose Gardner Investigations
Neely Kate Mystery
Darling Investigations
Carly Moore

Romance:
The Wedding Pact
Bachelor Brotherhood
Off the Subject

Find out more at
denisegroverswank.com

Find out more about
Christine Gael's books
at
christinegael.com

DENISE GROVER SWANK

NEW YORK TIMES BESTSELLING AUTHOR

A N D

CHRISTINE GAEL

finding
peace

Bluebird
BAY

This book is a work of fiction. References to real people, events, establishments, organizations, or locations are intended only to provide a sense of authenticity, and are used fictitiously. All other characters, and all incidents and dialogue, are drawn from the author's imagination and are not to be construed as real.

Chapter One

W e're out of fruit and cottage cheese. And make sure you don't get the peaches packed in water this time. They taste like somebody ran 'em through the dagnab dishwasher, for crying out loud."

Stephanie Ketterman swallowed a sigh and turned toward Pop with a forced smile. "You know that Doc Richardson doesn't want you having a lot of added sugar. You're already borderline diabetic, Pop. If you don't like the peaches, why don't we try fresh strawberries?"

"Because the seeds get stuck in my dentures, if you must know, Miss Goody Two-Shoes. Always wanting to rat me out to my doctor," he harrumphed. "And if I wanted strawberries, I'd have asked for them."

Her father crossed his arms and glared at her through bloodshot, bleary eyes, and she said a silent prayer for patience. He clearly hadn't slept well the night before and was out of sorts. She'd fight this battle when she got back from the grocery store. Hopefully by then he'd have squeezed in a nap and forgotten all about it.

One more month. Thirty days until the in-law addition she'd commissioned would be complete and she'd have her life back. Or at least somewhat. Between her sisters' help in the evenings and the new daytime nurse Pop had hired after the sale of his newly rebuilt beach bungalow, she would only be required to spend two evenings a week with him. After a solid eight months of having him directly underfoot, she couldn't wait. It wasn't so much the lack of privacy or his presence—she'd come to terms with their tenuous relationship the previous year after nearly losing him and some subsequent major heart-to-hearts with her sisters. She'd taken stock of her part in their issues and they were closer now than they'd ever been. But there was no denying it. Pop, who was cantankerous on his best day, had been struggling with the early signs of dementia, and the disease had made him even more thoughtless and sometimes downright cruel. She felt for him, she truly did, but empathizing with his illness didn't take away the pain of his words some days.

And lately, her skin seemed thinner than ever.

Because you're hiding your head in the sand, Stephanie. You know what you need to do.

She scrubbed a hand over her face and turned back toward her father, choosing the lesser of two evils for the moment.

"Was there anything else you needed from the store?" she asked cheerily.

"Nope. Not unless you come across a pretty blonde who wants to help an old man cross the road or something."

She turned away wordlessly and made her way out of the living room and into the kitchen. The weekday nurse, Judith, gave her a sympathetic smile from her perch at the island, where she was mixing Pop's oatmeal with Metamucil.

"The night nurse texted me early this morning and warned me that he had a rough one. Nightmares about the fire. He's a bit out of sorts, so I'll make sure to baby him a little today. I'm making his favorite chicken salad with apples and walnuts for lunch. Oh! And I brought over *The Quiet Man* on Blu-ray for us to watch. Don't rush back, okay?" she added gently. "Maybe go window shopping on the pier or stop by the bakery and see Cee-cee...It's Saturday. Take some time for yourself."

The weather had finally turned over the past few days and not only had the last of the snow finally melted, they were on track to hit sixty degrees before noon. Maybe a visit with her oldest sister and a walk along the pier in the sunshine was just what the doctor ordered.

She sent Judith a grateful smile, making a mental note to pick up a half dozen cupcakes to send home with the nurse. Cee-cee had just created four new flavors for spring, including a raspberry and white chocolate concoction that Stephanie couldn't wait to get her hands on.

She'd just snagged her purse and reusable shopping bags for the grocery store from the pantry when her cell phone trilled with the ringtone she'd programmed for emergency calls from her veterinary practice.

She dug the phone from the pocket of her jeans and pressed the green button to answer.

"Dr. Ketterman speaking."

"Oh, thank God, Stephanie. I thought you were closed on Sundays," muttered a panicked male voice, "It's Bryan Perkins."

"Hey, Bryan. So good to hear from you," she said, frowning as she set her purse down and leaned a hip against the kitchen island. Bryan had been college roommates with Paul. Since then, he'd remained one of her husband's oldest friends and longtime business partner until his death. He'd been almost as devastated as she had been when Paul had passed. More than that, he'd been irreplaceable in the weeks following. He'd put his whole life on hold to not only help her with mundane things like hiring someone to mow the lawn each week and coming over to clean the gutters after a storm, but also to help her with important matters like navigating the muddy life insurance waters that had seemed too overwhelming and sad to deal with at the time.

They'd spoken less frequently over the past year or so, as the Earth continued to turn despite Paul's absence, but they'd stayed in touch, meeting for lunch every few months or one of them calling the other for a quick check-in. Even then, he'd always contacted her through her personal cell number or on her home phone.

"Why are you calling on the office phone?"

"I didn't want to bug you if you were actually taking a Sunday off to relax, but if you're in the office anyway, I'd really appreciate it if I could swing by with Pepper." His normally warm voice was stark and shaky. "Apparently, I didn't push the dining room chair in all the way after breakfast, and he managed to climb onto the table and get into a box of chocolates a client gave me. I woke up to a shredded, empty box and a whimpering Pepper. I'm really worried about him."

Last time she talked to Bryan, a few months back, he'd told her about his new rescue, a three-year-old, energetic Boston terrier. Pepper had been neutered and had all his shots before the adoption process, so she hadn't expected to see him until the end of the year for an annual exam and booster shots. She'd seen pictures of Bryan with the dog on Facebook, and both looked totally smitten. Ever since Bryan's amicable but difficult divorce a few years back, Stephanie had worried he'd been a bit lonely, so she was thrilled he'd found a companion to hike and share his love of the outdoors with, even if it was the four-legged variety.

Needless to say, she didn't hesitate, restructuring her day in her mind. "Aw, poor Pepper! Were the chocolates dark or milk?"

There was a long pause before he replied. "Looks like what's left of the box says milk chocolate. Is that important?"

"It's actually better, yes. None of it's ideal, obviously, but milk chocolate is less dangerous than dark. Depending on how much he ate and kept down, this could turn out to be nothing. Head on over to the office now, Bryan, and bring the box with you. If I'm not there when you get there, just hang in there for a few minutes. I'm leaving the house now. Try not to panic, okay?"

"Wait...this is your office number, right?"

"Yup. I have that number patching into my cell phone on Sundays unless I schedule a surgery for a critical client or something."

"Geez, Steph, don't let me wreck your one day off. I can call the animal hospital over on Market Street."

"Absolutely not," she shot back quickly. "I won't even hear of it. I'm hanging up and heading out, so don't even think about blowing me off now. See you in a few."

She disconnected, not waiting for a reply. When she unlocked the doors to her office a short while later, she was relieved to find that she'd beaten Bryan. It would give her time to fire up the coffee maker, check on Shelley the turtle, and prep to treat Pepper. As always, a feeling of warmth and belonging filled her as she took in the sights and smells of the office. A lot of vets kept the furnishings utilitarian, but Stephanie had always wanted her clients and their pets to feel comfortable, especially since many were visiting under duress. There weren't rugs or upholstered chairs, but the walls were a soft blue and photos of pets on the beach on bright sunny days adorned the walls. Paul had helped her make her dream come true, but it was all hers, and the style reflected her personality through and through. Soon, though, she would be sharing the place when her son Todd came back home after graduating from veterinary school. There was no denying the place had a feminine tone—would Todd want to change it? Was it wrong that her heart bled a little at the thought?

Too many changes. Too much transition. It seemed like an avalanche lately...

Sarah was getting married and Todd was coming home. Her oldest sister Cee-cee had gotten divorced, opened a cupcake shop, and found a wonderful man who appreciated her fun-loving side instead of squashing it. Her younger sister Anna had been diagnosed with breast cancer, and although she had a great prognosis, she'd faced an elective double mastectomy to make sure it didn't return, and was undergoing chemo and radiation. Thankfully, she'd given up traveling for her photography career and was working at a conservation center while undergoing treatment and recovery. Stephanie only hoped Anna's new love interest, Beckett, would be strong enough to keep her footloose sister home for good...or at least a whole lot more than before.

But despite everyone else hurtling toward the future at warp speed, Stephanie felt stuck. Paul had died more than two years ago, and while she'd finally begun to move forward, albeit by inches, she kept encountering things that held her back—Paul had a secret, and she had no idea what it had been about. Or rather, she suspected but couldn't bring herself to go there. Because what if Paul hadn't been the man she thought he was? What if he'd been having an affair?

Her entire life felt like a lie.

Bryan phoning up unexpectedly felt like serendipity. Maybe it was a sign that it was time to poke this wound a little and see if there was something to her suspicions. First and foremost, though, Stephanie hoped poor Pepper would respond well to her treatment.

To that end, she began prepping supplies.

The front door opened a few minutes later and Bryan walked in holding his black and white dog in his arms. She took one look at the dog's lethargic demeanor and Bryan's worried face, then ushered them into Exam Room One, which she'd gotten prepared for their arrival.

"Thank you so much for meeting me, Steph," Bryan said, setting the dog gently on the exam table before raking a hand through his golden blond hair. "I wasn't sure if . . ." His anxious voice trailed off.

"You did the right thing," she said. "Let's look poor Pepper over."

Stephanie was pleased when the dog's heart sounded even and strong. Her lungs were clear and her pupils were reactive. Bryan placed his hand on the dog's back and rubbed behind her ears while Stephanie conducted her exam.

"I brought the box," Bryan said, patting his jacket pocket.

"That's a good sign that it fits in your pocket," she said with a smile.

Sure enough, it was a small sampler box that was wet and mauled.

"Pepper really wanted in that box," she said with a laugh as she took it from him.

"She loves to chew things."

Stephanie nodded as she read what was left of the nutrition label, but enough was there to reassure her. She opened the lid and saw indentations for six pieces, or so she guessed based on the size of the box and what was left. "The good news is that I think Pepper will be fine after I treat her. It was definitely milk chocolate and there were only a half dozen pieces. And since Pepper's on the large end of a Boston terrier, her size helps dilute the amount of theobromine and caffeine in her bloodstream."

"So I ruined your day and brought her in for nothing?" Bryan asked sheepishly.

"No…" She shook her head. "Definitely not for nothing. As a precaution, I plan to induce vomiting before I send her home with you, and then you'll need to watch her for any signs of seizures, or restlessness. Or if she starts repeatedly vomiting or has diarrhea. Then I'll have you bring her back in."

Fear filled Bryan's hazel eyes, and Stephanie placed a hand on his arm. "I don't expect you to see any of those things, but I need to warn you nonetheless."

He nodded.

"Let me take Pepper into the back and take care of the dirty business."

He nodded, still looking worried but a little more relieved.

Scooping Pepper into her arms, she carried her to the back. It took her nearly fifteen minutes to induce vomiting and then get the activated charcoal down her, but when she carried Pepper back to her anxious father, the dog had definitely had her fill of Steph.

"She should be good to go," Stephanie said as she set the squirming dog down on the floor. She ran behind Bryan's legs and stared up at Stephanie with suspicion.

Steph figured she deserved that.

"If there's anything I can do to repay you for the emergency visit," Bryan said, "please feel free to ask."

Stephanie leaned a hand on the stainless steel exam table. "Well, actually . . ."

Bryan's face lit up. "Name it."

She doubted he'd be so eager to help after she asked her question. "It's on the serious side," she prefaced.

He sobered and stood up straighter. "Okay."

Biting her lower lip, she wondered how to ask. Did she just blurt it out? Did she state her evidence? A note that he was meeting someone and a receipt for a breakfast she hadn't known about on the day of Paul's drowning at sea...not exactly condemning, except that Paul and Stephanie shared everything about their lives. She practically knew how many times he went to the bathroom throughout the day. Which meant the note and receipt were huge. She'd never rest until she knew the truth. Good. Or bad.

"Bryan," she said in a serious undertone. "Do you know if Paul was having an affair before he died?"

He gave her a blank expression, then glanced around. "Are there cameras? Am I being pranked?"

"Bryan, I'm serious."

"And so am I," Bryan said, his gaze piercing hers. "Paul loved you with every fiber of his being. How can you ask such a thing?"

She nearly confessed about the suspicious evidence but then stopped herself. She was being foolish and paranoid. She was dishonoring her husband by even considering such a thing. She could only imagine how hurt she'd be if she'd been the one to die, and Paul had begun questioning her fidelity.

With a tight grin, she said, "It's nothing." She rubbed her forehead. "Just crazy thoughts."

"I'll say. That man loved you with a devotion I've never seen before." He lowered his voice. "And if I'm honest, that's part of the reason Misty divorced me. Because I didn't love her enough. I didn't love her like Paul loved you."

"Oh, Bryan," she gasped in horror.

He chuckled. "Please. It's fine. Our marriage was over years ago, and it had nothing to do with you and Paul and everything to do with me being a workaholic." He bent over and picked up his cowering dog. "There are three things I know with certainty—the world is round, the sun will rise in the east, and Paul Ketterman loved his wife."

"Thanks," Stephanie said, hanging her head in shame.

Bryan started to leave the room, then stopped and turned to face her, his expression solemn. "It's okay to move on, Steph. Paul would want you to, I promise. You don't need to vilify him to give yourself permission."

Then he left without another word.

She stared at the door long after he left, mind reeling.

Dear Lord...Bryan hadn't sugarcoated it, had he?

Deep down, she knew he was at least partly right. Paul *did* love her and he *would* want her to move on. So long as she knew that, what did the rest of it matter? Who cared if he had a breakfast she didn't know about one time, or met a friend on the pier? She needed to just let it go, once and for all.

Because vilifying her near-saint of a husband in order to give herself permission to move on?

That would make her a monster.

Chapter Two

One hundred forty-seven, one hundred forty-eight, one hundred forty-nine, one fifty. Done!"

Cee-cee Burrows looked up at her sister Steph, who sat at the worktable across from her, and blew a chunk of freshly cut bangs from her eyes and swiped her hands down her apron.

Cupcakes were baked, filled and cooled, and she'd counted and recounted them at every step of the process, making ten to spare, just in case. Now to decorate, and she'd be able to deliver them first thing tomorrow morning for the grand opening of the new teaching hospital in the center of town. Dr. Epstein, Anna's surgical oncologist, had been invited to become part of the team there and had recommended Cee-cee's shop to handle the dessert. But Cee-cee owed him a far greater debt of gratitude than just that. He'd given her youngest sister a new lease on life, and her health back. Cee-cee had offered to do the cupcakes for free, but he wouldn't hear of it. At the very least, she had to make sure she did him proud and that they came out perfect.

She stretched her aching back and took a seat on one of the stools she sat in to decorate. There was a lot to do, and if she didn't put her nose to the grindstone and start now, she was going to be in the weeds by afternoon.

She'd just finished filling her piping bag with Italian buttercream when the dumbwaiter sounded, kicking her into action.

She stood and bustled over, swinging the door to the dumbwaiter open. She'd expected the usual—a note from her part-time employee, Pete, letting her know they were low on this or that flavor, or with a new large order to fulfill for the following day. Instead, she found a stunning bouquet of yellow roses surrounded by sprigs of lemon leaf and baby's breath.

"Oh!"

Tears sprang to her eyes as she leaned in to take a long whiff. The heady scent filled her nose and she plucked the creamy white card from the cheery nest of blooms.

Just wanted to thank you for the best eight months of my life.
All my love,
-M

She blinked back the tears and lifted the vase from the dumbwaiter, grinning like a fool. Had it only been eight months? Sometimes it felt like forever ago that she and Mick had gone from friends to so much more. Now his life was so interwoven with hers, she couldn't imagine it any other way. She made a mental note to run to the grocery store after the shop closed. He loved her pistachio-encrusted rack of lamb with couscous, and he deserved a romantic treat of his own when he got home.

Whoever said it took a village was right. She was proud of herself and her accomplishments, but she knew full well that the support of her family and loved ones was a gift that never stopped giving, and made her heart feel full every single day.

"Those are absolutely stunning," Steph said in amazement.

"I'm so lucky to have found him," Cee-cee said. "I never take him for granted."

"You deserve every bit of happiness you find with him, Cee-cee."

"Thanks."

"I think this calls for a short coffee break," Steph said, jumping up from her seat and making a beeline for the coffee pot. She poured their coffees, then returned to the worktable, two steaming mugs of coffee in hand.

Cee-cee was smiling contentedly as she made her way back and picked up one of the large coffee mugs with both hands. She took a grateful sip of the coffee—extra strong, just how she liked it—and let out a satisfied sigh.

"Perfect. Thank you."

"No problem," Steph murmured as she set her own cup down and gathered up the wafer paper, scissors, and other supplies to make the sugar flowers like it was second nature.

"So what's on the agenda today? Anything fun planned?" Cee-cee asked, scooping up the piping bag and settling to work.

"I'm going to head down to the pier and do some shopping. Maybe even start looking at mother of the bride dresses for Sarah and Oliver's wedding."

"If you try anything on, send pictures so I can help you pick," Cee-cee replied, shooting Steph a warning glare. "You know you'll wind up choosing something frumpy if Anna and I don't keep an eye on you. And with your figure, especially now with all the yoga, you really should find something that skims your curves instead of something oversized. You don't want Anna badgering you after the fact."

Cee-cee half wondered if her sister's penchant for loose-fitting clothes allowed her to be more invisible. That preference had only seemed to come about after Paul's death. Like if another man admired her, it would be a betrayal somehow.

The thought cascaded into more disturbing thoughts, and Cee-cee pushed them away.

"Or, you can wait until Tuesday and I can go with you? Mick has been pressing me to pick a day off that I stick to in hopes of making sure I don't burn out, and Tuesday is the slowest day at the shop."

"Okay, I'll probably still go window-shop today just to spend some time out of the house, but maybe we can go together again and try on Tuesday," Steph replied as she very studiously focused on her petal-cutting technique.

"Everything okay?" Cee-cee asked, cocking her head as she eyed her sister more closely.

"Yeah, fine, why?"

Steph's reply was light and airy, but the second Cee-cee stopped what she was doing and really looked at her sister's face for the first time today, she knew something was wrong. People always said eyes were the windows to the soul, but Steph was a whole lot easier to read. While Anna could be a mystery and inscrutable at times, Steph's expressive features laid bare her every emotion no matter how hard she tried to hide them.

"What's going on?" Cee-cee asked softly. "Is Pop okay?" She searched Steph's dark eyes, anxiety creeping up the back of her neck like a snake.

18

"Pop is…Pop," Steph replied with a forced smile. "He's fine. Irritating, cantankerous, often rude, and demanding. So, you know, the usual. And I'm okay. Nothing new or earth-shattering, I swear," she added hastily at Cee-cee's dubious look. "I just…I had a weird encounter with Bryan that sort of took the wind out of me."

Steph paused and took a sip from her own cup as she lowered herself into the bench across from Cee-cee.

"His new rescue, Pepper, got into some chocolate this morning, so I met him at the office. The poor pup is fine," Steph hurried to clarify as Cee-cee let out a pitying gasp. Steph was an amazing vet, but she definitely took her job to heart and wept for each and every lost patient, which might have explained her mood. "Irritated with me for making him throw up and probably a little uncomfortable, but he'll make a full recovery. It was more the conversation I had with Bryan that has me feeling off."

A strange heat shot through Cee-cee as she settled back into her seat. Something that felt a whole lot like guilt.

"Oh?" she asked, hoping her voice didn't sound as strained to her sister as it did to her own ears. "And what was that about?"

Maybe it was nothing to do with Paul. Maybe Bryan had asked her on a date or had done something else that made Steph feel uncomfortable. But the second they locked gazes, she knew that was just wishful thinking. The only thing that would rock her sister back on her heels like this was new information about Paul's death. Or worse, his life.

Steph looked up from the flower she was fashioning and shrugged. "Do you think the reason I can't stop thinking about that stupid note and the Pietro's receipt is because I'm trying to give myself permission to move on, and the only way I feel like I can do that without hating myself is if I somehow smear Paul's memory?" Steph looked away, her throat working as she swallowed hard, clearly near tears. "Like, if he wasn't as amazing as I remember...if we weren't truly soul mates, then my heart can let go of him and forget him?"

Cee-cee took a sip of her drink just to have something to do with her hands, but the coffee that had seemed so delicious only moments before went bitter in her mouth as she tried to keep her face impassive.

"Oh, Steph, I don't think that sounds like you at all. You loved Paul to pieces. Everyone who knows you two knows that. And it will have been three years in a few months. Who would judge you for moving on with your life at this point?"

"That's the thing, Cee-cee," Steph replied, looking miserable. "I would judge me. Deep down, I feel like letting Paul go is a betrayal. But if I had a good excuse, like maybe he was cheating on me? That he wasn't really the man I knew and loved? Then it's okay, right? I can go on with my life and just set that all aside."

Cee-cee's stomach pitched as she tried to parse her words carefully. "I don't think that sounds like you, Steph. If you're worried that you have some subconscious desire to see Paul in a bad light that isn't justified, maybe speak to a grief counselor or therapist? I'm sure that's something many people go through, or at least wonder about. You're not alone. So many people have lost their spouses, I'm sure there is someone else in your shoes right now. Anna loves her cancer support group for exactly that reason. They give her something that, no matter how much we love her, we can't offer. True empathy. Complete understanding of what you're going through. Maybe that could help you as well. We lost Mom together, but that's different than losing your spouse

20

and father of your children. Especially given the bond the two of you had."

Steph bit her lip and nodded slowly. "I guess so. And maybe I'll try that. Because, if I'm being totally honest, I can't stop thinking about it all. The note, the receipt. I try to put it all out of my mind, and sometimes, when I'm really busy at work or talking about wedding stuff with Sarah, it works for a while. But at night, when I lie down in bed…our bed? It comes rushing back again. Bryan says it's nothing. To stop thinking about it and let it go. He's the one who said that maybe this was my way of trying to move on, but that Paul loved me like crazy and would never cheat. Surely he would know, right? I mean, friends since college? Co-worker? He'd know, wouldn't he?"

She didn't want to lie to her sister. They'd never deceived one another before and she wasn't about to set a new precedent now. But she still wasn't sure what to do with the knowledge she'd recently acquired. Who knew how accurate it was? And even if it was accurate, it might not mean anything. If these worries and concern about Paul's past were already keeping her sister awake at night, adding to that would only make it a thousand times worse. For what? Just to ease her own conscience?

No.

Until she'd thought about it some more and weighed all the pros and cons, she couldn't justify blowing up Steph's whole world over what very well might be nothing. Maybe it was time to talk to Anna and see what she thought. Cee-cee had resisted up to this point, despite almost a week having passed since the disturbing conversation, because her youngest sister was just on the tail end of dealing with her own nightmare. But now that her health was stable and she was no longer in constant discomfort from her surgery, maybe it was time to share the burden and get her thoughts on the matter.

A plan of action decided, Cee-cee focused back on Steph, reaching in to take her hand.

"Yes. I would think if there was something nefarious to know, Bryan would know it," Cee-cee replied carefully. "But I still think you should find a professional to talk to."

If this all turned out to be nothing like Cee-cee hoped and Bryan had implied? Great. Steph could still use someone to talk with to help her through the grieving process that she'd been struggling so mightily with for the past couple years. And if Cee-cee decided to tell Stephanie what she'd learned and they followed that lead to find out that it *wasn't* nothing? Then she'd have established a relationship with a professional who would surely have her hands full with a truly devastated, broken woman in need of help and comfort.

"I'll look into it. I'm sure there is someone good my GP can refer me to in the area," Steph said with a nod, seeming to feel slightly better at the thought. "It probably really is for the best just to put it to bed, once and for all. In the dark of night, when it gets really bad, I've considered doing things you wouldn't even believe," she admitted with a wince.

"Try me," Cee-cee said softly.

"Like having a handwriting expert look into the note to see if there was a match somewhere on some mystical database. Contacting our creditors and banks to get old statements mailed to us for the year prior to his death to try to find anything suspicious, like hotel meetups or more restaurant bills. I mean, who am I, freaking Veronica Mars?" she groaned. "Cee-cee, I went to Pietro's last winter to grill the staff about a breakfast from two years before. Who does that?" She shook her head and blurted out a semi-hysterical chuckle. "A woman on the edge, I'll tell you. What was I thinking? Some waitress was going to be like, 'Why yes, funny you should ask! I *do* recall seeing your dapper husband with some floozy on the day of his death some random weekday morning.' It's ludicrous. Both because they'd never remember, even if they did still work there, but also because that wasn't Paul, was it?"

Steph shook her head fondly, her features going soft with the memories of her husband.

"Heck, he didn't even like going out to lunch with his assistant Lydia because he didn't want to give people the wrong idea." She smacked her hand on the table between them and straightened. "You're right. Enough is enough with this nonsense. It's been months since I found that note and I've let it drive me crazy for too long. I'll talk to a therapist, and who knows? Maybe she'll have me doing something badass and symbolic, like set the receipt and that note on fire, and I'll have some sort of epiphany and finally be free of this ridiculous suspicion."

Cee-cee's throat was too tight to reply and she took another sip of the rapidly cooling, bitter brew clutched in her numb hand.

She'd pushed for this. Had wanted it. And now that she'd gotten her way, she realized exactly how wrong she'd been. The only secret that had ever come between her and her sisters had been when Anna had kept her diagnosis from Cee-cee. Despite the fact that Anna's cancer was gone and would hopefully never return, that moment had left a mark on Cee-cee's heart. She'd been so preoccupied with her own life, Anna hadn't felt comfortable sharing her most soul-deep pain with her. Cee-cee would have to live with that for the rest of her life. Things were good between them, and they were as close as ever, but Cee-cee would never forget the lesson she'd learned.

Personal growth and taking care of one's self was important. Imperative, even. Putting Pop, her ex, her kids and everyone else first had nearly broken Cee-cee. But going too far the other way could truly hurt the people she loved. Even now, when she thought back on how she'd nearly pushed Max away, she shuddered. Her job and her outside interests were the air she breathed. But family was the foundation of her life. The very earth she walked on. And secrets destroyed families. Just look at what Paul's secret was doing to Stephanie, and he was long dead.

God, but she hated to hurt her sister…

She had to sit back and really assess this situation carefully. On the one hand, she could pretend she'd never heard what she'd heard. She could go on, let Steph work through this all in therapy and stay none the wiser. And sure, maybe she'd do great and the suspicions would never rear their ugly heads again.

But what if they *did*? Skeletons always seemed to have a way of rattling in that closet no matter how dead they seemed. If things did come back to haunt them, then Cee-cee would be left having to explain that she'd withheld information from her sister. Information that could've changed everything.

She stared at Steph's bent head, face screwed up in concentration as she fashioned the petals on her latest flower.

There was no choice here. Cee-cee had been fooling herself to think there was. Steph deserved the truth, no matter how much turmoil it might cause. There would be no secrets between them, come what may. Now she just had to figure out the best time and place to tell her. A quiet place. A place of solace and peace. A place where she could fall apart completely.

Because if Stephanie's beloved husband had an affair? Everything Steph knew and believed about her whole life was a lie, and it was going to tear her heart in two.

Chapter Three

Anna Sullivan couldn't believe what her sister was considering.

"Absolutely not!" Anna Sullivan said, shaking her head vigorously to get her point across and nearly stumbling. Cee-cee had called and asked her to come over as soon as she got off work at the conservation center so they could go for a walk on the beach, saying she had something important to talk about. Anna had thought it might be about Pop, or Cee-cee's daughter's failing bookstore. Never in her wildest dreams had she considered this. *Have you lost your mind?*

"Secrets only tear us apart, Anna," Cee-cee said as they walked along the beautiful Maine coastline. The air was crisp and clouds gathered in the east, looking dark and ominous as the sun set to their left. Spring had technically sprung, but winter still held tight some days, its bite in the wind.

"Actual secrets," Anna protested. "Not *gossip*. There is no way we're telling Steph this. It would devastate her!"

"Don't you think she has a right to know?" Cee-cee asked. "I know you had your reasons for not telling me about your cancer diagnosis, but it hurt more than you realize. Secrets only tear us apart," she repeated stubbornly.

Anna cringed at the reminder. Cee-cee had been in the middle of a baking contest and busy with her new life and boyfriend. Anna hadn't told her for a host of reasons—some selfish—but now she could see how it had hurt her sister's feelings. While Anna could understand why Cee-cee had been hurt, gossip and insinuation that Stephanie's deceased husband was possibly having an affair before his death wasn't even close to being the same thing.

"I'm sorry I didn't tell you last December, and I truly regret it," Anna said. "But this is something else entirely. Stephanie and Paul had the perfect marriage. The type of marriage all others aspire to. You saw the two of them together. There was no faking that. How can you even consider this to be true?"

"Because Prue Simmons isn't a gossip. She doesn't take joy from hurting other people or stirring up trouble, and she's not prone to exaggeration. So for her to bring it up means there's something there, Anna." Then Cee-cee added, "Besides, we both know that Steph already suspects."

Anna shook her head. "No. She let it go when she brought it up before Christmas. We convinced her that there was no way he'd cheat on her."

"But she didn't let it go. It's been tearing her apart." Cee-cee stopped and turned to fully face her sister. "Did you know she went to the restaurant she found that receipt for, hoping to get answers? She can't let him go, and now she's beating herself up with guilt because of her suspicion. This past weekend, she asked Paul's old business partner, Bryan, if Paul had been having an affair."

Anna's mouth dropped open. "What? She called him?"

Anna prayed Steph hadn't shown up to his office with the inquiry.

"No," Cee-cee said, waving off her questions. "His dog ate chocolate and Bryan brought her in to the clinic. She asked him then." Her brows shot up. "The point is, it doesn't sound like she's letting it go."

Anna started to walk again, trying to figure out what to do. "What did Bryan tell her?"

"That Paul had been faithful."

"Well, there you go," Anna said, relieved. "Nothing to worry about."

"Oh, please," Cee-cee said, rolling her eyes. "I've met Bryan before and he's just like Nate—oblivious to everything that doesn't directly affect him, which means he likely would have been clueless if Paul was having an affair."

Anna was quiet for several long seconds, the sounds of the surf slowing her anxious steps. There was no doubt that Steph had been stuck in her grief, but adding to her suspicions about Paul having an affair seemed like a bad idea. "Okay," she said with a sigh. "Tell me exactly what this Prue person said and why you believe her."

Anna had heard the name before, but being in and out of Bluebird Bay all these years herself, she really had no notion of the woman's character.

Cee-cee's back straightened as though she was bracing herself to tell the story. "I hadn't seen Prue for years. She moved away shortly after Paul died. She was in town visiting her mother and had heard about my cupcake shop, so she stopped in. We'd spent several minutes catching up when she said she was sorry to hear about Paul's passing. I told her we were all very upset since it had been so sudden. I told her that Steph was having a hard time getting over his loss. Then Prue gave me a strange look."

"And that's when she started gossiping," Anna said with a frown.

"No, she was confused. She said she thought that Paul and Steph's marriage had been on the rocks."

"See?" Anna said. "Gossip."

Cee-cee shot her a glare. "After quite a bit of coaxing, she finally told me that she'd seen Paul having breakfast at Pietro's with another woman. They were sitting in a private spot, leaning their heads together and whispering. Prue said she'd planned to stop over to say hi until she realized the woman wasn't Stephanie. She said she was surprised when she saw his obituary the next week and realized he was still married."

Anna shook her head, her stomach churning. "I don't believe it for a minute. How can we be certain it was Paul?"

"The timing's too coincidental," Cee-cee said. "A breakfast meetup at the same restaurant right before his death? And Prue knew him. Anna, it was definitely Paul." She sounded bitterly disappointed.

Anna was quiet for nearly a minute. "Is now really a good time? With Sarah's wedding and Todd coming home to help Steph run the practice? So many big life changes." She grimaced. "Cee-cee, Steph's never handled change well. How do you think she's going to handle this? Not to mention all she has going on with Pop. Maybe we should wait. Give her a little time to settle into a routine with Todd at least . . ."

"Steph is beating herself up, wondering if she's imagining everything and villainizing him so she can move on. We need to tell her. And soon."

Anna slowly nodded, an ache filling her chest. Cee-cee wasn't an alarmist. If she felt like there was something fishy going on, then there probably was. This was going to devastate Steph.

"Okay," Anna said. "We'll tell her. Together. And we'll be there to pick up the pieces." She gave Cee-cee a sad smile. "Because that's what sisters do."

Chapter Four

P lease tell me you're just kidding."

Stephanie did a little twirl and eyed her older sister questioningly. "What's the problem with it? Navy is classic any time of year, the cut is elegant, and the price is right."

Cee-cee gestured to the dress with a sigh and turned to Anna, brows raised. "A little help here?"

Anna held up an "I got this" hand and rose from the seat in the corner of the oversized dressing room.

"First off, *The Price Is Right* is the name of a game show, not your mantra when buying a dress for your only daughter's wedding. Second, if you want a dress in navy, or you want a boring, ankle-length cut with no pizzazz, that's fine. Pick one or the other, but you're not leaving the store with both. You look like you're trying out for the part of Mrs. Doubtfire or something. It's really just dreadful and sad looking."

Leave it to her baby sister to give it to her without even a granule of sugarcoating.

Stephanie groaned and faced the mirror, trying to see the dress through fresh eyes. "Is it really that bad?"

Granted, the loose-fitting A-line didn't exactly compliment her figure. And maybe the navy did make her look a little pale...

Anna held up a finger and shoved a hand into her jeans' pocket before pulling out her phone and holding it to her ear.

"Hello? Yes, I'll tell her. Okay, bye."

Stephanie cocked her head suspiciously. She hadn't even heard the thing ring...

"That was Nana Sullivan calling from the grave. She wants to know if she can borrow that dress when you're done with it," Anna deadpanned.

Cee-cee broke into a fit of giggles as Steph propped a hand on her hip and shot Anna a mock glare.

"You are seriously too much, invoking our sweet, deceased granny to make fun of your older sister."

"She would approve...of both the joke and that dress. Which is how you should know to put it back on the rack. She thought the nuns' habits showed too much skin. Come on," Anna wheedled, pocketing her phone to free her hands for wringing and pleading. "Give me one crack at it and I promise, if I fail, I'll leave you to it."

Who was Stephanie kidding anyway? Once Anna got her mind set on something, it would take an act of God to stop her. It was a trait that had served her well in both her career and her recent health crisis, so most times Stephanie was grateful that her sister was so doggedly determined.

Today was not one of those times.

Stephanie blew out a sigh, shot one last glance at the mirror, and nodded. "Fine. You can each pick out one dress for me to try. One!" she added, holding up her index finger for good measure.

"With no caveats. Anything we want," Cee-cee pressed, going for the jugular.

When they'd picked her up that morning, she'd laid out the ground rules right from the start. Nothing sleeveless or too flashy color-wise, and no cleavage. Anna had balked instantly. Sarah didn't plan to have an overly formal event, and being that it was going to be held in the middle of summer at an open-air venue near the beach, Anna claimed that sleeveless seemed almost mandatory. Stephanie had put her foot down, explaining that, despite all the yoga, she still had too much jiggle. Now, though, what did it matter? Only her sisters would see her in their choices anyway. It wasn't like she was going to select one of them. Hell, she'd let them dress her up in a naughty French maid costume if it would shut them up and let her do her own thing once she'd appeased them.

"Whatever. Go for it. No holds barred. Bring on the latex!" Stephanie said with a sweep of her hand.

Her sisters squealed with glee and nearly tripped over each other spilling out of the dressing room back onto the boutique floor.

Stephanie shut the door behind them and leaned against it with a groan. She was surprised to realize she was actually smiling. Granted, they were testing her nerves, but the three of them all being together never ceased to lift her spirits. And, despite her best efforts, her spirits were a mess lately.

"More than lately," she muttered under her breath as she pushed away from the door and began to shimmy out of the ugly navy dress.

Nothing had been good since Paul's passing. The five stages of grief had stopped dead at number four. She'd apparently just decided to relive the previous ones, over and over, like her own hellish version of *Groundhog Day*, instead of moving on to the acceptance stage. Since her talk with Bryan a couple days ago, though, she'd been stuck firmly in the depression and isolation camp. If she could have, she'd have locked up the practice, climbed into bed, closed the blinds, and lain in bed watching *Golden Girls* reruns for the foreseeable future. Her responsibilities hadn't allowed her to commit that fully, though, so she'd settled on the bare minimum. Canceling her early morning yoga class on Monday, bowing out of dinner with Sarah, and stripping her patient schedule down as much as possible. It was only her sisters' combined insistence that she not blow them off today and the knowledge that they would badger her mercilessly if she did that had made her come.

As much as she hated to admit it, she was glad she did. They'd kept her mind off Paul and her whole talk with Bryan and had given her a much-needed respite from her own brain, which seemed intent on producing every guilt-inducing thought possible.

How could she have let a silly note and some dumb receipt let her doubt her wonderful husband? What did that say about her as a person? And as a wife?

"Open up!" Anna's muffled voice sounded through the door as she banged on it for good measure. "I've got *the one*."

Stephanie swallowed back the lump of emotion lodged in her throat and took a steadying breath before tugging open the dressing room door.

"Okay, Miss Fashionista, let's see it."

"I don't claim to be a style icon," Anna said with a chuckle, "but I know colors and I know lines. You're going to be a knockout in this."

She held up the dress slung over her arm, and Stephanie stared down at the cloud of royal blue chiffon.

"Oh, Anna, I don't know. . . ," Stephanie said, shaking her head slowly.

"Good thing you don't get to decide since this is my pick. You promised to at least try it on," Anna said as she tugged the dress off the velvet hanger.

"Do mine first!" Cee-cee called as she burst into the room. "You're going down," she crowed at Anna as she held up her hanger like it was a first-place trophy.

This one was a little less flashy, in a shade of apricot similar to the color Stephanie had painted her bathroom. Both dresses were sleeveless, and both were tea-length as opposed to being long, but she had to admit, they were both lovely.

"You have exquisite taste. And if I was hip and cool like you guys, I'd probably be all over one of these. But you know I'm more of a Dorothy than a Blanche, so seriously, don't get your hopes up," she warned, reaching for Cee-cee's choice first. If she was going to pick one of them, it was the more likely of the two.

She slipped it on over her bra and underwear and turned her back to her sisters. "Zipper's in the back. Can you do me up?"

Cee-cee complied and then grabbed her by the shoulders to steer her back around, facing the mirror.

"Your figure looks amazing," Cee-cee said, eyes gleaming with excitement and what looked suspiciously like tears.

"You seriously do," Anna admitted grudgingly. "It's very flattering."

Stephanie tried not to focus on her bare arms, instead homing in on the positives. Anna was right. The dress was a trim-fit from top to bottom and skimmed her curves nicely but wasn't too tight in a way that made her feel self-conscious. Still, the color made her look a bit sallow and tired.

"I don't know, maybe with a bit of a summer glow it would be all right?"

Cee-cee frowned and slumped forward, dejected. "I love the cut of it, but I have to admit, you're right. It could be a better color for you. Try Anna's now."

Stephanie shot the dress a dubious glance and then trained her gaze on Anna, who was already shaking her head.

"Don't even think about backing out."

Stephanie grumbled as she turned to let her sisters help her out of the apricot dress and into the royal blue one.

"I'm older than you, you know," she reminded Anna a moment before she was summarily stuffed into a wad of chiffon. "You shouldn't get to boss me. It's supposed to be the other way around."

"Yeah, well, tough cookies, toots," Anna replied, the smile clear in her voice. "I was born with a bigger mouth than you. Now turn around and let's see it, shall we?"

Stephanie turned, hand in front of her face as she peeked between her fingers.

The sight that greeted her made her heart give a hitch.

"Well, I'll be damned," Cee-cee murmured as Anna let out a low whistle.

"I. Am. A. Genius."

But Stephanie barely heard them. She'd been hurled back in time, to thirty years before. They had gone to a fancy holiday party at Paul's boss's house after receiving an official invite to the event on fancy stationery with silver foil-embossed calligraphy. She could still remember the hors d'oeuvres being passed around on gleaming trays by tuxedoed waitstaff—fat, succulent prawns glazed in sweet and sour sauce, buttery scallops wrapped in bacon, and petite, single-bite lollipop lamb chops that had melted in their mouths. She and Paul had sipped from crystal flutes of golden champagne and giggled like children who'd gotten away with some mischief in the corner. It had seemed like such a grown-up thing to do after spending most of their college years eating Top Ramen and drinking wine from a box after a rare night out at the two-dollar drive-in.

But what she remembered most was Paul's face when she'd walked into the living room/dining room of their cramped one-bedroom apartment in the chiffon dress she'd bought at a secondhand store.

It had been black, not royal blue, and the sheer, fairy-like fabric had been a ludicrous choice for that time of year, but she'd felt like a princess in it. And, judging by her husband's expression, she looked like one too. All night, he'd had a hand on her bare upper back or slung around her waist, like he couldn't keep his hands off her. More than once, she'd caught him watching her from across the room as she chatted with some of the other guests, and each one of those times, she'd thanked her lucky stars she had a man that looked at her that way.

"I'll take it," Stephanie said, blinking back tears as the memories faded and she focused on her reflection.

"Yes!" Anna shouted, pumping her fists as she turned to Cee-cee. "In your face, sucker!"

Cee-cee rolled her eyes as she continued to beam at Stephanie. "I can't even be mad. It's perfect on you."

"Thank you. Paul would've loved it. He always said this color blue looked amazing with my hair, and I think the style would've tickled him." Part of her wanted to share the memory with her sisters, but the larger part of her wanted to keep it tucked away…another diamond in the treasure chest that belonged to her and the love of her life alone. "I'll get a shawl for the church ceremony, though," she added primly with a smile. But as she waited for at least Anna to argue with her, she realized that both of her sisters had gone suspiciously silent. "What's the matter? Is it the arms?" she asked, taking off her rose-colored glasses mentally and giving herself a more critical once-over.

"No, no, honey. Your arms are great," Cee-cee said softly. "The dress is absolutely stunning on you. The bodice fits you like a dream and the swingy skirt is perfect for dancing. You're so right...Paul would've loved it."

Anna nodded mutely and the two sisters exchanged a glance in the mirror.

"That's it," Stephanie said, wheeling around to face them head-on. "What the heck is going on here? We were all laughing it up, you guys were teasing me relentlessly, and now suddenly you two start acting like we walked into a morgue. What gives?"

Anna wet her lips and eyed Cee-cee pointedly. "Steph...Cee-cee has something to tell you."

Cee-cee's eyes went wide as she glared at Anna. "Seriously?"

"Well, I mean, it is your story, right?" Anna said, cheeks going pink as she turned away from Cee-cee's icy glare.

"Technically, yes, but we said we were going to tell her together after a nice lunch—"

"Enough!" Stephanie said, the warm feelings bubbling inside her suddenly turning to ice. "Someone better tell me something right now, or I'm going to kill you both. You're scaring me."

After all the tough and often sudden news they'd dealt with in the past eight months or so, from Cee-cee's husband leaving her to Pop's house burning down to Anna's illness, they'd all had enough surprises to last them a lifetime. Cee-

cee nodded and sucked in a breath before letting it out in a rush.

"Steph, I don't know how to say this to you, or if I should be saying it at all, but I spoke to someone who knew Paul and had seen him just prior to his death."

The room seemed to sway and tilt as beads of sweat pearled instantly on her upper lip. The sense of impending doom was so strong it made her knees buckle.

"Okay...who?"

"It was Prue Simmons. You remember her, she used to work at the bank years ago? Her father was an auctioneer?" Cee-cee babbled aimlessly.

"What did she say?"

Those were the words that came from Stephanie's lips, even as her heart murmured a totally different sentiment with every beat.

Don't say it.

Don't say it.

Don't say it.

"This might not mean anything at all, Steph," Anna cut in before Cee-cee continued.

"But she said that she saw Paul out for breakfast at Pietro's on the day of his death."

"And?" Stephanie swallowed hard and waited for the other shoe to drop.

"He was with another woman...and, um." Cee-cee eyes filled with tears and one broke loose, coursing down her cheek. "They looked...close."

Close.

Close.

Physically close? Close as in laughing like old friends...or giggling like new lovers?

"Close, how?" she heard herself whisper.

She didn't know she'd asked the question out loud. In reality, Prue Simmons and her impressions didn't matter all that much in the scheme of things, because whatever Paul had been doing, he hadn't trusted his wife enough to share it with her. That was the most devastating blow of all.

"Close enough that she had thought…assumed that he was no longer married."

A groan worked its way out from deep inside her as she began to weave, her legs on the verge of buckling.

She'd been wrong. His lack of trust hadn't been the most devastating blow, after all.

Her beloved Paul—her soul mate and best friend—had been cheating on her, and her whole life was a lie.

Chapter Five

Cee-cee and Anna both sprang into action, catching Steph before she hit the ground.

"I should have waited," Cee-cee said, trying to remain in control and not freak out as she and Anna helped Steph down to the bench in the dressing room.

Anna shot her a dark look that suggested now was not the time to try to backtrack. Once they got her seated, Anna started fanning Steph with the hanger.

"That's not going to do her any good!" Cee-cee protested, instead reaching for Steph's head and pushing it between her knees.

Steph's face was buried in a cloud of fabric and she fought against Cee-cee's hand. "I'm suffocating in chiffon!"

Cee-cee jerked her hand back as though it was on fire. "Oh! I'm sorry!"

"Okay," Anna said, taking on the tone of a drill sergeant. "First we get that dress off Steph and get her back into her clothes. Then we're headed to Gino's for pasta and wine." She lifted her hands when Cee-cee and Steph started to speak. "This calls for carbs and alcohol. I'm buyin'."

Steph's lip quivered and she was dangerously close to breaking down. Cee-cee wondered if taking her out in public was a good idea, but Steph stood and lifted her chin. "I'm due for a cheat day."

Then she realized what she'd said and broke into tears.

The two sisters quickly removed the dress from Steph and got her own clothes back on. Cee-cee and Anna gave the gorgeous blue dress a long look, then left in on the return rack. There was no way Steph could wear a dress that would remind her of her husband's infidelity at her daughter's wedding. She wanted to karate chop Anna right in the throat for bringing it up at exactly the wrong moment. At the same time, she couldn't blame her. Once Steph had started talking about Paul, it had been hard to control their expressions and play it cool. She'd known something was up.

But what a mess.

Cee-cee felt even more guilty than before. "Would you rather just cancel dinner?" she asked once they were in the parking lot.

Steph turned to her with a tear-streaked face. "Part of me wants to go home and bury myself under an afghan while eating a tub of Ben and Jerry's and watching *The Time Traveler's Wife*, but I've spent the past nearly three years doing that. I'm done mourning a man who turned his back on his marriage vows at worst, and kept more than one secret from me at best." She turned to Anna, who she had to know would back up her decision. "I need wine. Pronto. And pasta. Let's go."

Anna seemed more certain about this plan than Cee-cee, so certain she snatched Cee-cee's keys and opened the rear passenger door, practically shoving Cee-cee into the back. "Don't overthink it, Cee-cee. Just go with it."

"You just want an excuse to eat pasta after your doctor put you on that low-carb diet," Cee-cee grumbled.

Anna let out a forced-sounding chuckle. "Busted. Now get in the car because Gino's toasted ravioli are calling my name."

Steph got into the front passenger seat without a word, staring straight ahead.

Cee-cee still wondered if this was a good idea. If she was Steph right now, she'd want to be alone, at home, crying her tears, but Steph had a point. She'd cried gallons of tears. Maybe she needed something different. And being alone seemed like the last thing she needed.

They were all quiet on the drive, but Anna snuck a few worried glances at Cee-cee in the rearview mirror, making Cee-cee feel better that Anna was just as worried.

When they got to the restaurant, Steph got out first and walked right in, not waiting for her sisters. By the time Cee-cee and Anna had caught up, Steph had already requested a table and a pitcher of sangria.

"Steph?" Cee-cee asked. "Maybe . . ." Her voice trailed off at the determined look in Steph's eyes.

"We're eating pasta and drinking wine. Sit."

"Okay."

They sat at a table overlooking the ocean, and Cee-cee couldn't help thinking the turbulent waves mimicked her sister's emotions. Had she made a terrible mistake by telling her?

The waiter brought the pitcher as he came to introduce himself. "I'm Allen and I'm going to be your waiter tonight. I heard there was a sangria emergency."

He looked doubtful that such a thing existed.

"Yep," Anna said, snatching the wine from his hands, as well as one of the glasses.

He gave Anna a wry look as she poured a generous amount into the glass and shoved it at Steph.

"Drink." Anna shot him an expectant look as she took the other two glasses. "You might as well bring out another pitcher and an order of toasted ravioli."

Steph had taken a long gulp of her sangria and lowered her glass to say, "And bruschetta." Then she glanced at Cee-cee and added, "Plus an order of mozzarella sticks, to start."

"Okay," the waiter said, looking a little leery. "I'll go get that order in and grab a few menus."

Anna quickly passed a full glass to Cee-cee, then poured herself one.

"A toast," Steph said, holding up her nearly drained glass.

Cee-cee gave Anna a horrified look, but Anna shrugged and held up her glass. Cee-cee reluctantly lifted hers as well.

"To the truth," Steph said, her voice breaking. "May it set us free."

"Oh, Steph," Cee-cee gushed, tears flooding her eyes.

"Drink," Steph said as she reached for the pitcher.

Anna snatched her glass and filled it up, then handed it back.

Steph took another generous sip, then said, "I know you're upset, Cee-cee, but you have no idea how free I feel now. I can let go of all of that guilt I've harbored for months, thinking he had an affair, then beating myself up for even considering it." She shook her head. "I'm glad you told me. This is great. Perfect."

"You could have picked better timing, though," Anna said dryly over the top of her glass. "What a waste of a beautiful dress." Then she leaned forward, her eyebrows rising. "And just for the record, I still won the dress competition."

"Really, Anna?" Cee-cee asked in disbelief, but Stephanie started to giggle.

Cee-cee turned to her in shock, half-expecting her tears to turn to sobs, but Steph just laughed and finally caught her breath enough to say, "She's right. She won."

Ah, so it was starting to make sense. Her sister was clearly in the numb-zone. Cee-cee considered trying to get Steph to take a step back and process the whole thing, but maybe denial was okay for tonight. The pain and realization would come soon enough...

Cee-cee rolled her eyes, downed the rest of her sangria in one drink, then held up her glass to Anna. "If you can't beat them, join them."

Anna grinned ear to ear.

When the waiter returned with the menus and a fresh pitcher, they had already polished the first one off. "Wow...maybe you should have headed down to the Crab Shanty for their $2 margarita night."

"Oh!" Steph said, her eyes wide with excitement. "Maybe we can go there next."

Anna burst out into laughter and snatched the menus. "Lighten up, Albert. My sister just found out her dead husband cheated on her."

"Actually, it's Allen, and—" His eyes widened with horror as he turned to Cee-cee. "Wait, can ghosts have affairs?"

Cee-cee fought hard to keep from laughing as she said in a serious voice, "Did you never see the movie *Ghost*?" When he gave her a blank look, she added, "You know that movie with Demi Moore and Patrick Swayze and Whoopi Goldberg? Never mind. Anyway, Patrick was a ghost and had an affair."

"With Whoopi Goldberg?"

"No, with Demi Moore. There was clay involved…Look, the important part," she said with more emphasis, "is that it was based on a real story." Then she gave a definitive nod to add credence to her story.

The waiter looked horrified. "I'm so sorry."

"As you should be," Anna said. "You can repay us by bringing us a slice of tiramisu."

"Right now?" he asked. "Before your main course?"

"If there's ever an occasion for tiramisu as an appetizer, a cheating ghost is it," Anna said.

He nodded and scuttled off.

"You've scared that boy for life," Steph said with a giggle. "And Patrick wasn't cheating on anyone with Demi in that movie."

"Of course he wasn't," Cee-cee said as she took another sip of her wine. "But that boy will never figure it out."

They broke into another round of laughter. Then Steph turned serious as she grabbed Cee-cee's hand. "I know you feel guilty, but I'm glad I know. I'm relieved." Tears swam in her eyes. "I thought I was going crazy."

"You're not crazy," Cee-cee said, but a new guilt replaced the other. She'd known Paul for over thirty years. He just didn't seem the cheating type, but then again, neither had her own husband. But after Cee-cee had found out, she'd been able to look back and see the signs. He'd put more care into his grooming and clothing. He'd disappeared for long periods of time. He'd grown distant. As far as she knew, Paul hadn't exhibited any of those signs. Did that mean he hadn't cheated? Or had he hidden it better than Nate? "But we're still not sure Paul was cheating. I just needed you to have all the information."

"Now I have it. And no matter what, Paul was sharing a cozy meal with another woman that I didn't know about. He's guilty of something, Cee-cee. And frankly, I don't care what right now. He lied to me, both by omission and in fact when he told me he was going fishing when he was really going on a breakfast date with another woman. So no frowning," Steph said, then reached her hand to Cee-cee's forehead, using her finger and thumb to smooth out her frown lines. "They might get stuck and then you'll look old and get traded in for a newer model."

"Too late," Anna said, pouring more wine into her glass. "Cee-cee already got traded in, but it worked in her favor. She traded up from a Subaru to a Lamborghini."

Steph lifted her glass. "To my future Lamborghini."

The women broke out into a fit of giggles. The wine flowed freely as they dined, until they'd gone through three pitchers and were nearly falling out of their chairs in their fits of giggles.

A man in a dress shirt and tie walked over and towered over their table. "Ladies."

Anna buried her chin to her chest, then tried to mimic his deep tone. "Gentleman."

The three burst into laughter.

A grin tugged at his mouth, but he tried to look serious. "I'm sure you all are having a great time, but I wanted to advise you that there's a law against public intoxication."

Steph snorted and tried to plaster on a serious face. "Then you should tell some people who are publicly intoxicated."

His grin tugged even harder and he lifted his hand to cover his mouth for a few seconds before he squatted next to their table and said in a hushed tone, "I think I already have."

They guffawed again, and he waited patiently for them to regain control again. "Are you ladies celebrating?"

Anna started to pick up her nearly empty glass, then reached for the empty pitcher. "I think we need a new one." Her arm shot into the air and she waved vigorously. "Edwardo!"

"I think his name is Armen," Steph said, her forehead wrinkled in confusion.

"No," Cee-cee said, trying hard to be the voice of reason. "I'm sure his name is Arnold." Then she hiccupped.

"It's Allen," their waiter said again with a tight smile as he walked up to the table. "Though all three of you have called me anything but that tonight." Then, upon realizing how much money they had spent and likely thinking of his tip, he added, "Not that I'm paying attention or anything. Call me whatever. It's cool."

"We need another pitcher," Anna said, pointing to the empty one and missing, her finger poking the flower stem in the middle of the table. Petals fell onto the white tablecloth.

Allen made a face.

"Allen," the man said with a grim smile as he stood. "I'm cutting them off."

"You can't do that!" Steph said in outrage, shoving her finger toward the man.

"Actually," he said, slipping out his wallet and flashing them a shiny badge that read *Bluebird Bay Police*. "I can." He turned to the waiter as he repocketed his wallet. "Allen, they'll be taking the check."

Panic raced through Cee-cee's alcohol-drenched head. Were they going to get arrested? She pulled out her phone and sent a frantic text to Mick.

"It's not their fault," Allen said.

"God bless you," Anna said with a sharp nod.

"Her dead husband had an affair with a woman on a pottery wheel."

Cee-cee blinked in surprise. Had Alonzo googled the movie?

"Excuse me?" the officer asked, clearly trying hard to suppress a laugh. That was good. A chuckling man could hardly haul them to the big house, could he? Seemed cruel...

"Her dead husband had an affair," Allen repeated.

"Don't forget the pottery wheel," Anna said. "It's important."

The officer cocked his head. "Is that what they told you?"

"It's true," Steph said, narrowing her eyes. "I just found out my dead husband cheated on me." Her chin quivered. "I thought he loved me. He was my everything...and he...he . . ." Then to everyone's horror, Steph broke into tears.

Anna grimaced, then turned to the waiter. "Ah, crap. I was wondering when that was going to happen. Look, Ansel, we're gonna need a couple of boxes."

Cee-cee helped Steph to the ladies' room to get ahold of herself, leaving Anna to handle the bill. By the time they emerged, Anna and the officer were in the foyer, along with Mick and Beckett.

Relief flooded Mick's eyes when he saw her.

"We're getting arrested, aren't we?" she asked, then turned to the officer.

"No," he said. "Your sister explained it all to me with the help of your boyfriends. Under the circumstances, I think the best thing for everyone involved is to send you all home." He shot a grin behind him. "Especially since your sister left the waiter a very generous tip for his troubles."

Cee-cee nodded in relief, then wrapped an arm around Stephanie's back. "Let's get you home."

The officer handed Cee-cee then Steph a business card. "I'm Detective Ethan Jenkins. If you run into any more trouble, feel free to give me a call." Then he grinned at Mick and Beckett. "Gentlemen, I wish you the best of luck." Finally, he sauntered out the door, leaving them to deal with their strong, sweet, devastated sister and the wreckage her dead husband had left behind.

Damn you, Paul.

Chapter Six

P olly wanna cookie! Argh, Polly wanna cookie!"
"Oh my Lord, I will give you anything if you will just
stop squawking, Polly," Stephanie pleaded, her head
pounding like someone was using her skull as a bongo.
"Here," she muttered, handing the massive macaw an animal
cracker in the shape of a tiger. The bird took it daintily in her
razor-sharp beak and began to nibble in blessed silence.

Her afternoon drinking the day before had devolved
into a night of polishing off a bottle of wine at home in bed,
resulting in a hellacious Wednesday morning. She'd woken
up to a blaring alarm clock with a mouth that felt like it had
been stuffed with cotton and a splitting headache. It had
taken a half-hour-long shower, two cups of piping hot black
coffee, three slices of dry toast, and four aspirin to even
make an attempt to step outside the house into the relentless
spring sunshine. She'd wound up barely beating her first
client to the office, and had been running on fumes for the
past three hours with another five to go before she could
close shop and head home to lick her wounds.

And her wounds were deep.

"Oh, Paul," she whispered, blinking back the tears welling in her eyes.

Last night had been bad. The worst night she could remember since Paul had died, and that was saying something. Once she'd left the loving support of her sisters, assuring them she was heading to bed to sleep it off and needed to be alone, she'd found herself in a spiral of something so dark and terrifying, she was almost afraid to name it. It was only a text from her son Todd—just a random link to some silly animal-lover meme—that had stopped the self-destructive thoughts she'd been having in their tracks. She couldn't allow this new information to drag her under. Her children needed her. Her sisters and father needed her. She needed to find a way to claw her way back to the surface. By the time she'd closed her bleary eyes, she'd made a decision. A drunken decision, but one that sober Stephanie stood by.

There was only one thing worse than thinking Paul had committed the ultimate betrayal of their vows, and that was not knowing. It was time to end the worry, fear, and speculation and get to the truth—all of it—come what may. If that path led down a road to something terrible like decades of affairs or, God forbid, a whole other family or something equally nefarious, she'd deal with it. She'd lived her whole life and based her entire career on the old adage that knowledge was power, surrounding herself with books and journals and articles. When Anna had been diagnosed, she'd dove into the research and armed herself with as much information as she could because knowledge gave her a sense of control. And, when she was spiraling downward like an airplane shot out of the sky, control was everything. No more waiting for more secrets, whispers, notes, or receipts to emerge. She was taking the wheel, starting today.

The thought had given her the strength to get through the morning, albeit barely. The appointment she'd been waiting for was only five minutes away, and she found herself rehearsing what she planned to say once more.

By the time the clock struck noon and she'd gotten Polly safely ensconced back in her cage, all patched up for her owner to retrieve her, Stephanie was more than ready.

"Steph? You back there?" a low male voice called from the front reception area.

She'd hired a temporary receptionist to bridge the gap until Todd came on staff full time, at which point they figured they could man the desk well enough between them and a little bell with a "ring me for service" sign on it.

Stephanie bustled out of the treatment room and into the waiting area, where Bryan stood with a smile on his face.

"Hey there! You were right, he seemed totally fine to me," Bryan said, bending to pat the black and white pup on the muzzle. "Thanks so much for coming in on a Sunday for us the other day. I really appreciate it."

"No problem," Stephanie replied with a stiff smile. "Why don't you and that sweet boy come on back, and we'll just check his vitals for your own peace of mind?"

Bryan nodded, tugging a reluctant Pepper along as Stephanie led them into a second, empty treatment room.

"Has he been going to the bathroom normally? Drinking and eating well?" she asked as she closed the door behind them and lifted her stethoscope to her ears.

"Yup, all good. We spent yesterday evening playing Frisbee in the park and everything. He seems pretty much back to his usual self...but, are you feeling all right?" Bryan asked. "You look a little pale."

"I'm good. Just…a little too much cheer last night," she admitted ruefully, gesturing for Bryan to hold Pepper still as she listened to his heartbeat.

"Spring fever, I bet. It's been a long, brisk, and snowy winter, so I've been feeling it too. I hope you had fun at least," he said with a chuckle.

As much as she appreciated Bryan's easy acceptance of her worse-for-the-wear appearance, she couldn't take the easy out. Not when he'd offered her an opening for the very thing she wanted to speak to him about…

"Pepper's heart sounds strong, and he looks fit as a fiddle. You have nothing to worry about. As for me, it actually wasn't spring fever last night." She tugged the stethoscope from her ears and took a seat, gesturing for Bryan to do the same. "I know we talked about this the other day, and I truly don't mean to put you on the spot or make you feel uncomfortable, but I'm at a bit of a crossroads and could really use your help."

"Anything for you, Steph. Shoot," he said without hesitation, making her feel slightly less guilty about pushing him.

"Well, I know you said that Paul had never been unfaithful to me, to your knowledge, and I'm not doubting that you believe everything you said to me. But I've gotten some new information that suggests that Paul was…less than honest. Maybe with both of us."

Bryan drew back like she'd punched him in the chest. "What—what do you mean?"

"Well, one of my sisters—Cee-cee—spoke to a friend who saw Paul on the day of his death." Stephanie tried not to let the shame and pain drag her under, instead focusing on forcing the words from her mouth. "He was with another woman. They seemed very familiar, talking close and the like.

This was the very day he told me he was going fishing on the boat right when I was leaving for work. No mention of a meetup with a female friend, no mention of going to a restaurant at all. So I wondered if you can take a second, let that sink in, and then maybe think of anything Paul might have said or done that could be viewed as strange or suspicious, given that new information? Something that might have seemed innocuous at the time?" she added hurriedly.

If Paul had been cheating, he was the only one to blame. She didn't want Bryan to think she was accusing him of hiding her husband's infidelity. She just wanted to get to the truth.

Bryan took a long time to respond, and the tick of the clock in the background seemed to grow louder with every passing second. She couldn't deny that, deep down, she'd hoped he'd hop up in a fury and shoot holes in the story she'd relayed. That he would go on telling her how ludicrous the very idea of it was and this was her looking to demonize Paul again so she could move on.

But he did none of that. And when he finally spoke, each word was like a poison dart to her heart.

"I don't know, Steph," Bryan said, raking a hand over his face with a sigh as he shook his head. "I mean, I guess he was acting a little weird toward the end there. He missed a couple standing lunch and golf dates between us with little in the way of an excuse. I just assumed he was under a lot of pressure. We were juggling several projects at work, and there was a big merger on the horizon at the time. It didn't register that it might be something more than that, but it's possible . . ."

Stephanie cleared her throat and tried to focus through the headache that had only grown more intense. Concentrate on the facts. Pretend this is just some mystery you're watching on television that needs solving.

It was easier said than done, but she finally got her lips moving again.

"Was there a female colleague or someone he spoke to often or seemed close to?"

"He and Wendy Hoang were chummy, but I wouldn't say overly so. She's married as well . . ."

She'd met some of his co-workers through the years at various functions, but other than Bryan, he'd rarely socialized with them, so her knowledge of his work relationships was admittedly limited. She'd always had her own career to focus on, and it just hadn't seemed important to stay on top of the comings and goings at his office. Now, though, as she struggled to conjure up an image of this Wendy person, she found herself regretting her lack of knowledge.

"I can't say anything sticks out for sure, though. Did your sister mention what the woman he was with supposedly looked like? That might help jog my memory," Bryan said as he stroked an anxious-looking Pepper.

"She didn't, no. But that might be something I can have her ask."

Bryan cocked his head and studied her. "You sure you just don't want to drop it, Steph? Are you sure you even really want the answers to the questions you're asking? Maybe it's better to let Paul and everything the two of you had together rest in peace."

Stephanie stood, dashing at the sudden rush of tears sliding down her cheeks. "That's the thing, Bryan. I'm not at peace and I haven't been since the day he died. I need to see this through until I have the truth. Then maybe I can let him go. I understand if that doesn't make sense to you, and I won't bother you again with any of this. You have the right to remember Paul as a great friend…the man you knew and loved. Don't let me ruin that for you."

Bryan stood and stared down at her, his expression as solemn as a cemetery. "Not going to happen. He will always be that guy in my mind. It's because he was such a good friend that I refuse to let you do this alone. Whatever weaknesses he might have had and whatever he did, I know he loved you to pieces, and it would kill him all over again to see you torn up like this and hurting. If the truth is what you need to heal, he would want you to have it. That much I know for sure. So if you're intent on doing this, I'm going to do my level best to help. I'll ask around discreetly at work and see what I can find out. Let's stay in contact, and if you learn anything more from your sister that can narrow my focus, let me know, all right? I'm going to keep chewing on this all, dig up my old calendars and see if anything sets off alarm bells as being strange."

Stephanie bit her lip and nodded. "I will. And I appreciate this more than you know. Thank you, Bryan."

He smiled at her and blew out a sigh. "I'll talk to you in the next few days, then."

He let an eager-to-escape Pepper drag him to the door before the mean vet lady tried to make him throw up again. Stephanie watched as they filed out the door. When it was closed, she reached into her pocket and pulled out a crumpled business card that she'd somehow wound up in possession of.

Detective Ethan Jenkins.

Despite having cut them off, he'd actually been pretty lovely about the whole debacle of an evening, considering. She and her sisters had been fairly obnoxious, but once he'd heard the whole story, he'd treated them with kindness and sympathy. She'd already called the restaurant and apologized to their waiter, Allen, for their behavior. Once she'd climbed into bed the night before and the room had finally stopped spinning, she had planned to call the detective as well, to thank him. But since then, she had acquired another motive for her call.

She dug her cell phone from the deep pocket of her lab coat and punched in the number with a trembling forefinger.

"Detective Jenkins, what can I do for you?"

"Hello, Detective? This is Stephanie Ketterman. You, umm, didn't arrest me and my sisters last night for drunk and disorderly conduct?" she added hurriedly with a wince.

There was a long pause, and when he finally spoke, she could almost hear the smile in his voice. "Right, well, I don't think a ride in the paddy wagon was actually on the menu, but I do remember you, yes. Glad you made it home safe and sound."

"Thanks to you, we did. I wanted to let you know how much I appreciated your understanding. It's been a difficult time . . ."

"What with the pottery wheel and the ghost and all."

Her cheeks flamed and she slumped forward in her chair, trying not to let her personal shame derail her mission. "That part wasn't true, but the rest was, and I actually wondered if you might be able to help me on that front."

Another long pause.

"Okay, and how might I do that?"

She sucked in a breath and pulled the trigger, sensing deep in her heart of hearts that this was it. Once she set this series of events into motion, there would be no stopping it.

"I wondered if you did any detective work on the side. Like a private eye. I'm in need of one, and I'd like to hire someone with integrity. You clearly displayed that last night. What do you say? Will you be my Columbo?"

Chapter Seven

The next day was Steph's day off...not that she ever really had a day off.

After she got up—feeling a hundred percent better than the day before, at least physically—she made a pot of coffee and fed Pop breakfast. He was quieter than usual, staring at his oatmeal as though he wasn't sure if he liked oatmeal. It occurred to her that he may have forgotten what it was altogether, but she couldn't let herself go there. There was no denying his dementia was progressing, but they weren't to that scary place yet. It was more likely he hadn't slept well.

When the home health worker showed up, Stephanie checked her appearance in the mirror one more time and gave a slight nod. She didn't usually fuss over how she looked, not lately anyway. After her dress shopping trip, she realized she'd let a lot of things go. Especially her clothes. Comfortable was best at the clinic, but there was no denying she used to dress comfortably with more pizzazz before Paul's death.

It was time to start caring again.

She also admitted that she was dressing for her coffee date with Detective Jenkins. She shook her head, her cheeks stinging. Not a *date* date. Just a prearranged meeting to discuss investigating her cheating husband over coffee. Definitely not a date.

She'd never once considered dating anyone since she'd gone out with Paul on their own first date over thirty-five years ago. Could she even think about seeing someone else? Holding an unfamiliar hand? Kissing unfamiliar lips?

She shook her head. Where had this come from? Her limited recollection of Detective Jenkins was that he was attractive, but the odds were high that he was married. Did he have a ring?

Oh dear Lord, why was she asking herself if Detective Jenkins was married?

Her face flushed even more, and she fanned herself, telling herself it was just a hot flash. But now she looked over her appearance with a more critical eye. She was wearing tan legging pants with a black cardigan set and a pair of black flats. Her hair was blessedly still mostly auburn, but there were some silvery strands in the mix, and she self-consciously swept a loose strand behind her ear. Would a man even be interested in her at her age? She reminded herself that Cee-cee had found a good man and she was two years older. But Cee-cee was dating her high school almost-boyfriend. It was obvious that Cee-cee and Mick belonged together. They were soul mates.

And Paul had been hers. Or so she'd thought.

Pushing out a long sigh, she left her room and headed through the living room to the front door. Pop was sitting in a chair in front of the TV, looking listless.

"Maybe keep a close eye on him today," Steph said to his home health aide while trying not to worry. "He's much too quiet for Red Sullivan. I'm worried he's coming down with something."

61

"I will," she said. "There's a late flu bug going around."

Steph cringed, praying that Pop didn't get the flu. He'd gotten a flu shot last fall, but that didn't make him completely immune.

Worrying about Pop as well as her meeting with Detective Jenkins, she nearly missed her turnoff into her clinic. She didn't take appointments on Wednesdays anymore, reserving them for catching up on admin, which she planned to skip today, but she still had a few animals in the back that needed to be fed, watered, and peed.

She took out Fritz, a German shepherd puppy with an infected wound on his ear. His owners had gone out of town, and Steph had offered to board him while they were gone. He was miserable when she returned him to his penned-off kennel and promised to bring him home with her later that afternoon, not that he seemed to understand. After she fed and loved on a couple of kittens she was still trying to find homes for, she finally fed Shelley, the giant sea turtle she'd nursed back to health after his shell had been practically destroyed. She'd kept him since last summer, and he'd been ready to let go into the wild last November, but the cold Maine winters and the chilly Atlantic waters would have sent him into cold shock. So she'd kept him in the baby wading pool Anna's boyfriend, Beckett, had brought him, initially. Then, they'd upgraded to a pool that had been a water feature passed on from a landscaper client of hers. Shelley seemed content enough to paddle around, and she even occasionally hauled him out to roam the back of the clinic. Still, it was nearly time to set him free, and it made her chest constrict with anxiety. She'd planned to set him free all along, purposely not handing him over to the aquarium in Portland so he wouldn't live the remainder of his very long life in captivity. She'd intended to set him free, so why did a lump form in her throat at the thought?

After tossing him a generous helping of lettuce and carrots, she promised she'd return later when she retrieved Fritz, then hurried out the back door to her car. She'd dawdled far too long with the turtle.

This was one of the many reasons she'd never find another man to replace Paul. No one would understand and encourage her love for animals like he had.

Oh, Paul. Why'd you have to go and break my heart twice? Once when you died and the other when I discovered you were keeping secrets?

Traffic was terrible for some reason, and Steph was two minutes late when she pulled into the parking lot of Bright Eyes Coffee. She hated tardiness, and after the way Detective Jenkins had seen her two nights ago, she'd wanted to make a good impression, which was likely the real reason she'd been worried about her appearance. She was usually a normal person and didn't want him to think she was a drunken lunatic.

When she walked in, her gaze scanned the shop until they landed on the man who had flashed his badge at her and her sisters. He was dressed in plainclothes—jeans and a cable-knit sweater—and with his swath of wavy dark hair and athletic build, he was more handsome than she remembered, making her regret putting so much effort into her outfit. Would *he* think *she'd* think this was a date?

For heaven's sake, Stephanie. What man would think talking about your cheating dead husband was a date?

As she approached the table, she extended her hand. "Detective Jenkins, so kind of you to meet me."

He set his cup on the table and rose from his seat, towering a good six inches above her. "The pleasure's mine.

63

Please." He gestured to the counter. "Get your coffee. Then we'll chat."

"Can I get you anything?" she asked. "I see you have a coffee already, so maybe a bakery item? They have great pumpkin loaf here."

"I'm fine," he said in a warm voice. "Get your drink."

She ordered a cappuccino, which the barista made in what seemed like light speed, which meant the only thing left to do was sit down with Detective Jenkins. Why was she so nervous? It wasn't like he was going to slide a folder full of pictures of her husband and another woman across the table to her or something. He hadn't even agreed to accept her offer yet. This was a preliminary meeting only, and she needed to keep it together.

He smiled as she pulled out the chair and she sat in front of him, folding her hands on the table. "Thank you so much for meeting me."

He nodded with a small smile. "You already said that, and I'm more than happy to talk, but I feel like I need to be more forthright than I was on the phone." He paused. "Mrs. Ketterman—"

"Stephanie," she corrected, already tensing at his apologetic tone.

"Stephanie...I'm not a private investigator. And I'm limited in what I can do to help you in my capacity as a Bluebird Bay detective. I can only officially investigate your husband if a crime was committed."

"I'm so sorry," she said, her face flushing. "I wasn't thinking it through. I've wasted your time."

"No," he said, shifting in his seat and looking uncomfortable. "After seeing you with your sisters the other night . . ." He cleared his throat. "I wanted to help, so while I can't personally investigate, if you tell me what you know, then I can at least steer you to a good, reputable PI. They specialize, you know. So depending on what you're looking for, I can point you in the right direction."

"Oh," she said in surprise. "I had no idea."

"So tell me what you know, and what you're hoping to learn," he said, his warm, dark eyes full of empathy.

She took a deep breath and then let it all out. She told him about the note and the receipt and then how Cee-cee's friend Prue had seen Paul in the restaurant. She told him about Bryan's insistence he hadn't known, and reiterated their more recent conversation, where he said he'd poke around a little more at work. When she finally finished, she sat back and shrugged. "That's it. That's the whole story."

He listened patiently with kind eyes, then asked, "So what exactly are you looking for? What do you hope to find?"

"Proof," she said, her voice tight. "Irrefutable proof that he betrayed me with another woman."

He gave her a sad look. "I know that's what you think you want, but what good is it going to do? You didn't ask for my advice, but I'm going to give it to you anyway. You should let sleeping dogs lie and let yourself believe you had the happy marriage you thought you had."

Steph's anger rose. "That would be a lie."

"That *might* be a lie." His mouth pursed. "You really think finding proof your husband cheated on you is going to make you feel better?" he asked, not unkindly. But it still pissed her off.

"Are you married, Detective?"

He grimaced. "Not anymore."

"Divorced?"

He nodded.

"Wouldn't you have wanted to know if she was cheating?"

"I know for a fact she was," he said, a hard glint filling his eyes. "And I can tell you it wasn't exactly a picnic in the park."

Steph cringed, sorry for picking the scab off obviously still-fresh wounds. But her point was still a good one, and she pressed on. "So you're saying you would rather not know? You'd rather live oblivious to the fact?"

"That was different," he said, getting flustered. "We were still married."

"And in my mind, I'm still married to Paul," she said quietly. "I can't let him go and I can't move forward, especially now. Not until I know if my life was a lie."

"It wasn't a lie if you believed it was good. Truth is often about perception."

Was he right? She'd believed they were happy, so was her truth what counted? Had it been Paul's truth too?

She thought about all the sleepless nights and restless days she'd spent since finding the note and then the receipt...nights and days that had only gotten worse after finding out about what Cee-cee had learned.

"I still need to know," she said in a whisper.

He studied her for a long second then gave her a grim nod. "Okay, then." He leaned forward. "You got any paper to take notes?"

Relief washed over her and she eagerly got out a notebook and pen, ready to write.

"PIs are expensive, so you can do a lot of legwork yourself, then present it to them when you hire him or her," he said. "Since you have no idea who your husband met that day, you need to interview the people in his office, your old friends. Best-case scenario, they'll tell you straight off. If they

66

don't know, then maybe they'll tell you what they *do* know, like your sister's friend. Then you can start piecing things together.

"However," he said, leaning forward and lowering his voice, "You also run the risk of them not wanting to tell you directly. They won't want to hurt you, so it might be better to have your sisters ask."

"Or Paul's partner, if it's people at his job?"

He frowned. "Yeah. Him too."

Steph sat still for a moment, trying to sort through what he'd said.

"I know this is overwhelming, but having you or someone you trust ask seems less invasive and formal as opposed to having the PI do it. It could be a lot of interviewing and, at fifty to seventy dollars an hour, it will add up fast." An earnest look filled his eyes. "Stephanie, do you really think this is worth it? Wouldn't it be better to just move on and let the past be?"

"If my husband cheated on me, then my entire life was a lie," she said, holding his gaze. "If I have any hope of moving on, I need to know if he was with someone else. Was it a fling? Was he in love? Had he done this before?" Tears filled her eyes. "I've racked my brain, trying to look for the telltale signs that he was cheating on me, and God help me, I can't find a single one. The morning of the accident, he asked me to go out on the boat with him. Why would he have asked me to go when he was planning on meeting his lover for breakfast?"

Detective Jenkins shifted, looking uncomfortable. "I don't know. Maybe he changed plans?" He leaned in, head cocked to the side. "But I want to hear more about his accident."

"He went out fishing for the day and a storm came in. His boat was found in pieces, but Paul's body was never found."

"And this was nearly three years ago?" Detective Jenkins pursed his lips. "I think I remember that incident. Wasn't he an experienced boater?"

"He'd been on boats since he was a child," Steph said, surprised at his change in direction.

"If I remember right, that storm didn't just come out of nowhere," the detective said. "It seems odd that he was caught off guard."

"He knew it was coming in. He planned to be home well before it hit." In fact, she recalled not even being nervous about it at the time. She had speculated as to why he hadn't come in. Had his engine broken down? If so, why hadn't he radioed the Coast Guard? Had he gotten sick or hurt? Why hadn't he come in when he was supposed to?

Detective Jenkins nodded, looking deep in thought. Then he said, "I'd like to meet you again for coffee. Say next week? I'd like to hear about your progress and make suggestions for your investigation."

She narrowed her eyes in suspicion. "Why would you be interested in my husband's infidelity?"

"I'm not," he said with a teasing gleam in his eyes. "Maybe I'm worried I'll find you and your sisters drunk in public again."

Laughing, Steph glanced down and realized she had yet to take a sip of her coffee. "I assure you, Detective, that was a one-off. I don't make a habit of getting drunk, period, let alone in a restaurant."

He grinned, then sobered. "Still, I'd like to help if I can."

She wasn't sure why he would want to help but could find no good reason to turn him down, especially since he actually knew what he was doing. "Okay. Thank you."

"Don't thank me yet," he said. "You've got some sleuthing to do. And I'm still not sure you're going to be happy with what you find."

He was probably right. But she'd had happiness—or so she thought—with Paul. Now? She just wanted truth. Come what may.

Chapter Eight

C all me a stick in the mud, but I'm, like, ninety-seven percent sure this isn't what our sexy neighborhood detective meant when he said sleuthing around," Anna muttered under her breath as she and Steph stood in the cafeteria line of the Myer's Building, each of them with plastic, putty-colored trays in hand.

"Well, excuse me, this is my first time investigating my dead husband's possible mistress," Steph hissed, hitching the collar of her trench coat a little higher. "Sorry it's not up to your standards."

The line moved and they continued past the array of lunch offerings. The Myer's Building caterers weren't fooling around. They had everything from chicken marsala to pizza and pasta, not to mention a sweet-looking salad bar. Made sense, as the building housed half a dozen of the most successful businesses in town, including Paul's former business, accounting and financial planning firm, Perkins and Ketterman.

"I'm just saying, he told you to talk to friends, acquaintances, and workmates of Paul's. I don't get why all the cloak-and-dagger stuff," Anna replied, gesturing pointedly to the massive dark glasses covering half of her sister's face. "You look like a Kardashian trying to sneak out of a plastic surgeon's office without the paparazzi seeing them or something. Don't get me wrong, I'm all for costumes and hijinks, and I'm the last one to put the kibosh on…well, pretty much anything, but I think you probably could've just come in and talked to Bryan to see if anyone at Perkins and Ketterman fits the description of the woman Prue described to Cee-cee . . ."

"I already told you. I wanted to see if I could catch a glimpse of her myself first. After all, it seems like she's pretty distinctive looking."

When Prue had returned Cee-cee's call the night before, she'd apparently been super apologetic all over again for even mentioning what she saw at Pietro's. She hadn't meant to make Stephanie question Paul's fidelity, and wished she'd never mentioned it. But Cee-cee had quickly explained that other doubts had been raised since Paul's death and that she would be doing Steph a service by providing as much information as she could. Prue had reluctantly described the woman as attractive, in her early forties, with a mane of golden-blond hair that she'd worn in a thick braid down her back. Prue also mentioned that she'd had a distinctive birthmark above her lip. Anna had to admit, they'd seen a hundred or more women since they'd walked into this place, and none had fit the bill. Most of the women over forty had traded in very long hairstyles in favor of going shoulder-length or shorter, and the ones who hadn't were brunette. But she suspected the bigger reason her older sister had decided to try to find this woman on her own before discussing it with Bryan again was because she wanted to get a look at her first and do what any woman in the world would do.

Compare.

She was already younger, that much they knew for sure based on Prue's assessment. But was she prettier? Thinner? Curvier? Sexier?

What "er" was she that had been enough to make a man like Paul betray his vows?

And that type of flesh-flaying introspection was better done solo...

Or with your beloved sister, at any rate.

Anna kept those thoughts to herself, giving up on pressing Steph on the matter. What difference did it make why they were there skulking around incognito like something out of an episode of *I Love Lucy*? Her sister needed her right now, and if she'd asked Anna to dress up as Oompa-Loompas and go skydiving, she'd have said yes. Might as well buckle in and commit to the ride.

"Besides, you see the size of this place, right?" Steph continued as they approached the harried-looking person behind the grill taking orders. "We'll both have the chicken Caesar salad please," she said with an easy smile.

The woman adjusted her hairnet and began grilling two portions of chicken, not even giving Steph's semi-strange getup a second glance.

"It's massive. Bryan could've worked in this building with the woman for years and never noticed her. In fact, he seems like a bag lunch kind of guy and he's a workaholic. He probably doesn't even come to the cafeteria to eat."

Anna refrained from pointing out the fact that the breakfast-date mystery woman might not either, assuming she even worked in the building at all. Steph was almost manic with the need to do something while she waited for Detective Jenkins to get back to her with the name of a good PI, and this was just a reflection of that. The odds that they would run into this woman were extremely low, which was probably for the best right now. Her sister was one false move from shattering again, and Anna was seriously hoping Steph would be in a better emotional place if and when she did run into her. And on that note...

"Have you made an appointment with that therapist we talked about?" Anna asked gently as two plates of salad were slid across the glass case toward them.

"Not yet," Steph admitted, taking her plate and sliding down the line. "I've been really busy prepping for Todd to come in and all. I barely had time to slip out today for this," she added defensively.

"Right, but a phone call . . ."

"I have to do some research, find someone with good reviews, who has an office close to mine to make it convenient and all that."

Excuses. Steph was full of them. Anna got it—she'd been in denial when she'd gotten her cancer diagnosis as well. It had been the strength of her support group and the opportunity to lance that wound and let all the poison out that had freed her.

"You're swamped, so I'll take care of the research for you and short-list three candidates. I'll have it to you by the end of the weekend."

Steph was silent as they made their way toward the cash register to pay, and Anna wondered if she'd pushed too hard too fast. But when her sister stopped walking altogether, she realized Steph might not have even heard her because her focus was squarely on the back of a woman seated a few yards away. She wore a cheery cranberry-colored cardigan paired with a black pencil skirt. Her long golden hair was twisted in an intricate knot on the top of her head, held in place by a pair of gleaming black chopsticks.

"Steph," Anna murmured, watching in silence as her sister's paced quickened. She followed behind, pulse hammering.

Steph wound her way around to the front of the table, with Anna in hot pursuit. What in the world was going to happen if this turned out to be the woman they'd been looking for? She hadn't even pressed Steph on her plan of action for that event because it had seemed too unlikely.

Really…what were the odds?

The woman turned her head suddenly, her gaze sliding over Anna and lingering on Stephanie, looking her up and down with a puzzled frown before returning to her lunch companion.

Not her. The woman was lovely but couldn't have been a day over twenty-five and had no birthmark to speak of. Anna could almost see the air whooshing out of Steph as she turned away.

"This was silly," Steph murmured, her voice trembling as she led them toward a condiment bar that also housed plastic utensils and to-go containers and bags. "I don't know what I was thinking. I guess I wasn't. It's just driving me crazy knowing the answers I need are out there somewhere. It's like spending your whole life building an intricate puzzle, only to find that the last piece wasn't in the box. I can't think about anything else."

Her voice was shrill and she sounded close to tears.

"My greatest fear used to be something else happening to one of you guys, and it shames me to my core to admit that my greatest fear lately…?" She wheeled around to face Anna, her throat working furiously as she tried to get control of her emotions. "Is something happening to me before I get to the truth. I'm obsessed and it's grotesque."

"It's not, Steph. That's why you need to see someone. I guarantee this is a perfectly normal reaction to something so traumatic and life-changing, and a good therapist will tell you that. Please don't spend another second beating yourself up about it."

"I'll make the appointment as soon as I get back to the clinic," she muttered as she set her tray on the condiment bar and grabbed a to-go container. "Now let's get out of here before I make an even bigger fool of myself."

"Stephanie?" a low male voice called from behind them. "Is that you?"

Steph's eyes slid closed for a long moment before she pasted a smile on her face and turned.

"Heyyy, Bryan! Yup, it's me."

Anna stood back and watched the interaction between them, wincing. They'd almost gotten out of this little mess unscathed. She racked her brain to come up with a good excuse for being there dressed like Carmen Sandiego, but came up empty.

Luckily, Steph was a little quicker on her feet.

"I was actually coming by to see if I could talk to you for a quick sec, but then Anna realized she hadn't eaten lunch yet, so we decided to grab some food. This one, always on the lookout for her next meal," she said, elbowing Anna in the side.

Anna nodded and patted her belly. "Yup. Me hungry like Cookie Monster," she growled, playing along.

Judging by Steph's horrified frown, she'd oversold it, but whatever. If she wanted good acting, she should've given Anna the script. Improv was no joke.

"Are you okay? What's with the glasses?" Bryan asked, gesturing to the eyewear but also taking in the trench coat with a confused frown.

"Oh, I have a terrible case of pink eye. Like extra gross and drippy, so I didn't want to freak anyone out."

This was getting worse by the second, and Anna stepped between them. "Anyway, none of that matters. Do you have a quick second, Bryan?"

"For Stephanie? Always," he said, the cloud on his face disappearing as he gestured to a booth in the corner.

By the time they all took their seats, Stephanie seemed to have regained some of her composure. She leaned forward and patted Bryan's hand. "I'm sorry to just show up like this, but I wanted to ask if you'd gotten a chance to do any poking around yet about Paul?"

He nodded as he gave her hand a reassuring squeeze. "I have. And the more I poke, the more I think this is really a wild-goose chase. I'm turning up nothing. He was either very good at hiding it or he was exactly the man we both thought he was. Are you sure I can't convince you to let this go, Stephanie?" He shot a glance to Anna. "You saw them together. What are your thoughts?"

Anna paused with a forkful of salad en route to her lips and held up both hands. "I've already given Steph my two cents. I know Paul loved her. That much I can say without a doubt. But if she feels like she needs to pursue this, I'm behind her one hundred percent."

Because that's what sisters did.

"I have some new information that might help some," Steph said, settling back into her seat with a sigh. "The person who saw Paul at Pietro's that morning described the woman he was with." Steph went on to share the information Prue had given Cee-cee. When she was done, Bryan shook his head slowly.

"We have thirty people in our offices, and there isn't anyone that fits her description. Now, could she have been a temp, or work in the building at another company?" He shrugged. "Sure. But I feel like I'd have noticed a woman like that."

Steph glanced at her with a wounded look, and Anna wanted to kick him under the table. That was the last thing her sister needed to hear right now, a fact that seemed to dawn on Bryan right after he said it.

"Just because, you know, most women have dark hair. It's not like we live in Southern California or something."

Nice save, dum-dum, Anna thought with an approving nod as she dove back into her salad, happy enough to fill the role of the always-hungry sister to the best of her ability.

"Right," Steph said, setting her fork down with a sigh. "It was a long shot anyway. If you do think of someone who fits the bill, or hear anything you think I need to know about, give me a call. I'm going to just take a chill pill until Detective Jenkins gets back to me with the name of a PI who might be able to help."

Bryan blinked and swiped his mouth with a napkin. "Detective Jenkins? The police are involved in this? Why would they be? Paul's death was ruled an accident. Do we have some reason to believe this woman might have had something to do with it? Dear Lord...are you saying she could have been with him when it happened?"

Steph's face went chalky, and she realized that thought hadn't even occurred to her sister until now. Heck, even Anna hadn't considered that. But was it so outlandish to think that the woman he'd been dining with just hours before his boat went missing had accompanied him?

Anna made a mental note to ask Stephanie if the detective might be looking into a missing person that fit her description.

She refused to let herself get too carried away beyond that. But one glance at her shell-shocked sister told her that Steph hadn't done the same. She was firmly in the grip of another downward spiral as a whole new set of fears replaced the old ones.

What if Paul wasn't dead at all?

What if he'd faked his own death and had skipped town with his beautiful blonde mistress?

A piece of chicken lodged itself in Anna's too-tight throat as she tried to think of how to keep her sister from turning to ashes in this fresh hell. Because no amount of sangria in the world would dull the pain of a betrayal so complete.

Chapter Nine

"Max, I need your advice," Cee-cee told her daughter the moment she walked into Max's bookstore. "I've made a mess of things with your aunt Stephanie, and I'm not sure I'll ever forgive myself."

Max turned from straightening a stack of books on a display table and shook her head. "That's goes against all the laws of philosophy and science," she teased. "You're the most in-control person I know. And Aunt Steph is the most level-headed."

"I wasn't in control this time," Cee-cee said, juggling her pastry box as she shut the door behind her. "I opened a huge can of worms that I'd give anything to shove back in."

Max walked over and took the box from her mother. "I find it hard to believe that you made *that* big of a mess. What exactly did you do?"

Cee-cee's chin quivered. "I told your aunt Steph that Prue Simmons saw your uncle Paul having breakfast with a woman at Pietro's the morning of his death."

Max squinted her eyes shut, then opened them. "*What?*" Grabbing her mother's arm, she tugged her to the threadbare vintage Victorian sofa in the middle of the store and pulled her down next to her, setting the pastry box on the coffee table in front of them. "Maybe you better start from the beginning, because I think there's a lot more to this story than you're telling me."

So Cee-cee told her about Steph's suspicions and her conversation with Prue. "And now, Stephanie has resorted to staking out the Myer's Building cafeteria, looking for her dead husband's possible lover."

A lump formed deep in her throat and she willed herself not to cry.

Max studied her for a long few seconds, narrowing her eyes. "Let me get this straight. You guys find out that Uncle Paul was having lunch with a woman, and all three of you jump to the conclusion that he was having an affair?" She shook her head. Then horror filled her eyes. "Oh, my word. *Please* tell me Aunt Steph hasn't told Sarah, Jeff, or Todd any of this."

Max's reaction caught Cee-cee off guard. "No. She hasn't told them, not that I know of anyway. And it wasn't lunch. It was breakfast."

"Which is *sooo* much seedier," Max said, rolling her eyes. "After they spent the night together, *of course.*"

Irritation burned in Cee-cee's gut. "I can't believe you're taking this so lightly."

"And I can't believe you're taking it so seriously."

"Why is it so hard to conceive that Paul was having an affair?" Cee-cee asked, even though she'd struggled with the same thing initially. "Your father did."

Max leaned back and crossed her arms. "First of all, I love Dad, but he and Uncle Paul are completely different men."

Cee-cee couldn't disagree with that.

"And everyone who saw Uncle Paul with Aunt Steph knew they were the definition of soul mates. Sarah spent most of her middle school years completely grossed out by the fact her parents held hands and kissed in public. They chaperoned a homecoming dance while we were in high school, and she swore she was going to run away and start a life with a new name to escape the embarrassment."

"People change, Max," Cee-cee said with a sigh. "People fall out of love."

"Not Uncle Paul and Aunt Stephanie," Max said defiantly with an upturned chin.

Oh, to be so young and idealistic, Cee-cee thought.

"Look, Mom, all I'm saying is that you guys shouldn't be jumping to conclusions. You need to find out what was *really* going on."

Cee-cee cringed. "That's what we have been doing."

"No, you're looking to prove that Uncle Paul was cheating."

Cee-cee had to admit she had a point.

"Did you ever think maybe it was a business breakfast?" Max asked.

"No. Prue said Paul and the woman's heads were close together."

"Was the restaurant loud?" Max asked with a smug look. "Think about when you're at a noisy party and you're trying to hear someone talk. Don't you lean close?" She sat forward, placing her mouth close to Cee-cee's ear, and lowered her voice. "If you're talking about something important and want to make sure the person hears what you're saying, it might look a little intimate."

Cee-cee sat back and gasped. "Oh."

Max's eyes lit up in momentary triumph, then sobered. "Obviously none of you have tried to rule out that it was a business breakfast?"

"I don't see how it could have been," Cee-cee said. "Paul took the day off from work to take out the boat. He tried to get Steph to cancel her appointments at the clinic to go with him."

"My point exactly. Why would he invite her if he was meeting up with a mistress? Makes no sense, Mom."

"To cover his tracks? I don't know, Max." Cee-cee raked a hand through her hair with a sigh. "All I know is that he had a meeting. He would've told her about it unless there was a good reason to keep it a secret. Like an affair."

"Maybe it was last minute," Max said. "Has anyone checked his calendar? Or looked at his phone records?"

Cee-cee's mouth dropped open, and then she quickly closed it. "No. I don't think so."

Max shook her head and held up her hands. "Okay. I've heard enough. We're not discussing this any further until Aunt Steph and Aunt Anna are here."

"Anna?"

"Oh, *please*. You three are like the three amigos. If one of you is in the middle of something, the other two are in cahoots. Call your sisters and tell them to come to my apartment tonight at seven and we'll make a game plan. I'll make grilled chicken and roasted asparagus. If they have plans, tell them to cancel. We're nipping this fiasco in the bud."

CEE-CEE WASN'T SURPRISED when her sisters agreed to come to Max's that night, and she warned them that Max had a different take on things. At first, Steph was upset with Cee-cee for sharing the news with her daughter.

"I don't want Sarah to catch wind of this," Steph protested. "Not with the wedding and all. I don't want this tainting her memory of her father. She's in the process of creating a display with photos to honor him. This would kill her."

"Max doesn't want that either. Just come, Steph. Max has a different idea about how to go about finding out the truth."

Steph reluctantly agreed, mostly because she insisted she wanted the truth herself and could use all the help she could get.

Cee-cee showed up at Max's front door five minutes early, carrying a bottle of wine and a loaf of fresh bread from the local bakery.

"Dinner smells good," she said as her daughter greeted her.

Max took the wine from her mother and studied the label. "Good call on the wine. I picked up a bottle too. I suspect we're gonna need it."

Anna showed up a few minutes later, with her own bottle of wine, and Max laughed. "I hope Beckett's picking you up, because if we drink all this wine, you won't be able to drive."

"Beckett's used to being my Uber," Anna said. "I'm good."

Max took her bottle too and started to pour Cee-cee's Riesling for a predinner drink. Promptly at seven, the doorbell rang. Steph appeared in the doorway when Max opened the door. She walked in, the dark circles under her eyes making her look exhausted.

"I almost didn't come," Steph admitted as she walked through the door. "I think I'm losing my mind."

Max wrapped an arm around her aunt's shoulders and led her to the dining table at the edge of the living room. Anna and Cee-cee were standing at the head of the table, sipping wine.

"I'm glad you came, Aunt Steph," Max said, "because we're going to get to the bottom of this."

"That's what I've been trying to do," Steph said, tears flooding her eyes. "I made a fool of myself yesterday."

"I highly doubt that's possible," Max said, gently pushing her to her kitchen table. "But we're going to come up with a game plan that doesn't include you looking like a movie star trapped in the Myer's Building." Then she grabbed the empty wine glass from Steph's place setting and poured a generous helping.

"I'm not sure wine's a great idea," Steph said. "After last week . . ."

"Everyone's entitled to a little crazy," Max said, handing her aunt the glass. "Especially you, Aunt Steph. I suspect you've got a good thirty years of keeping your hair up in a tight bun, and you finally let it down."

"I haven't had hair long enough to put in a bun for years," Steph countered, picking up the glass and taking a sip.

"It was a metaphor, Aunt Steph, and your response only proves my point." Max went into the kitchen and grabbed the chicken and brought it to the table with the mushroom risotto and the bread Cee-cee had sliced.

When she sat down, Anna asked, "Okay, what are you cookin' up, kiddo?"

"Mom told me about the whole crazy idea that Uncle Paul was having an affair, and your attempts to find evidence it was true. But I propose we find out the truth objectively." She turned to Steph. "Aunt Steph, I love you, but you're too close to this to be effectively interviewing people. And even if by some weird alternate universe situation Uncle Paul was having an affair, do you really think anyone with any knowledge of it would actually tell you?"

Steph glanced down at the still-empty plate. "No. I suppose not."

"That's right, because they'd as soon as lie to you than hurt you anymore than you've already been hurt."

"Detective Jenkins suggested I hire a private investigator, but he also said the investigator would have to do so much interviewing that I could do some of the legwork, talking to people he worked with."

"And have you talked to anyone other than stalking people in the cafeteria?" Max asked.

"Well…no…"

Cee-cee was surprised to see her sister in a rare moment of embarrassment.

"What I'm proposing," Max continued, "is that we do an *actual* investigation. We can do some paperwork and internet sleuthing as well as interviewing people Uncle Paul worked with, but *you* won't be interviewing, Aunt Steph. You, Mom, and Aunt Anna will handle the paper trail, and I'll handle the interviews. I can ask the tough questions and not get emotional."

Cee-cee stared at her daughter, wondering when she'd become this strong, capable woman. "I take it you have a plan for us to dig into?"

Max grinned at her. "I do. I need Aunt Steph to call her cell phone carrier and ask for a detailed phone record of the month of Uncle Paul's accident and a few months prior. We'll go through and look for a pattern of phone calls or numbers you don't recognize. We'll also need Uncle Paul's debit card and credit card bills so we can look for unusual charges."

"And what are *you* planning to do?" Anna asked.

"I'm going to go up to Uncle Paul's office and start asking people if he was acting out of the ordinary before he died. I could be wrong, but I'm betting people will be much more likely to talk to someone who *isn't* Paul's widow. I'll definitely find his personal assistant and pump her for information. Then we'll take what we find and go from there," Max said. "Any questions?"

"Yeah," Anna said, pointing to the platter of chicken. "When do we get to eat?"

"Now," Max said with a laugh, then handed Anna the platter.

Stephanie looked like a weight had been lifted from her shoulders. Cee-cee knew her sister was relieved to consider another reason for her husband's odd behavior.

Cee-cee hoped they could get to the bottom of it sooner rather than later. Sarah's wedding was fast approaching, and this mess needed to be sorted out so a storm cloud wasn't hanging over the big day.

But more than anything? She prayed that they weren't getting her sister's hopes up for nothing. Surely Stephanie had suffered enough. And if Max was wrong? If Paul was somewhere drinking margaritas with some pretty blonde on an island somewhere, alive and well?

Cee-cee would kill him herself.

Chapter Ten

Stephanie stared down at the seemingly bottomless pile of papers in front of her and blew out a sigh.

So many phone numbers.

Hundreds of them. It had taken a few days to get the phone carrier to put them together and email them to her, and another few hours and two ink cartridges to print them all, but it was the tediousness of going through them, line by line, that was killing her. Luckily, Eva Hildebrand, friend, waitress and part-time caregiver, was at the house playing cards with Pop in his room and would be taking care of him all evening.

She'd started scanning through the ones on Paul's dedicated work phone first, beginning with the ones closest to the date of his death. Some she recognized, and most of the ones she didn't had the same seven beginning numbers, with different extensions comprising the last three.

All from Perkins and Ketterman.

None of them had been utilized on the morning of his death, and there was only one incoming call on his line at about eight a.m., from a number Stephanie recognized. It belonged to his assistant, Lydia.

Not early forties, not blonde, not slim, Lydia.

Could Max be right, though? Could that call from Lydia at the office have been one that had been the catalyst for the "sudden" work-related breakfast at Pietro's?

It was possible. Granted, it didn't seem likely. Stephanie and Paul were typically in constant contact throughout the day about work or the kids or whether one of them should cook or just pick up lobster rolls from the food truck in town for dinner. She would send him a picture of a dog X-ray with the clear image of a squeaky toy in its belly, and he might send her an article about some new supplement that was good for aching joints. If he was supposed to go fishing and plans changed, the only reason he wouldn't inform her with a quick call or text was if he was hiding it.

Or if it was an emergency of some sort . . .

She shoved the thought aside and tried to focus on what Max suggested. She wasn't looking for proof Paul was cheating on her. She was looking for anomalies. Anything out of the norm. And, most of all, she was keeping her mind open to any and all possibilities.

She'd highlighted Lydia's number in green and then jotted a little note beside it that read, "Lydia, Paul's assistant." That way, when she gave the call logs to Max for follow-up, she would know who she was looking for. Then she continued on, looking for any late-night calls or strange patterns and finding nothing.

Once she'd gotten all the way through to the previous year, she set those phone records aside and moved on to his personal line call logs, full of trepidation.

It felt a little like a violation of his privacy, and for the first time, she was glad his physical telephones had gone down with him on the boat. Going through it would've felt much the same, not to mention being emotionally devastating for her. Even looking at her own phone, listening to old voicemails and reading old text messages between them—some as mundane as "can u pick up milk on the way home," others as poignant as "Missing you today"— was heartbreaking. Scrolling through his phone as well, full of pictures and the like, would've laid her low for a week.

She picked up the first page and realized they were still stacked oldest to most recent. With a sigh, she began the process of sorting them as she had his work call logs so she'd be able to look at the ones nearest to his death first. It was only as she lifted the bottom sheet of paper and moved it to the top that she noticed something strange.

Adjusting her readers, she leaned in closer, certain the eyestrain was getting to her. But no, there it was in black and white.

More than a dozen missed calls from the same telephone number.

Four days *after* Paul's death.

Stephanie leaned back in the office chair, suddenly lightheaded. How could that be? Paul's phone had been lost at sea with Paul...hadn't it?

She leafed through the papers and, over the next half hour, managed to find that same telephone number fifteen more times. The first call had been an incoming one three months prior to Paul's death and had lasted nearly forty minutes. Others trickled in once a week or so from there. Some were placed by Paul, some were initiated by the mystery caller, but most were much shorter than the first call.

Most telling of all, though, was that the vast majority of them took place during the weekend.

Short calls to set up a quick tryst, maybe?

Stephanie sucked in a breath at the stab of pain and then pushed it away, forcing herself to focus on the bigger picture. If Paul's phone had been on him when the storm had hit, then how was he still getting calls? Granted, in her grief and shock, she hadn't had the wherewithal to cancel his service for weeks…maybe even months later, but if the phone was at the bottom of the Atlantic Ocean, how would it have even been able to register the calls at all?

An image of Paul wearing a fake mustache, his silvery hair dyed black as he lay stretched out on a chaise lounge with a pineapple-topped cocktail in hand, a leggy blonde beside him, filled Stephanie's mind and she nearly doubled over with the pain of it.

"Please, don't do this to me, Paul," she whispered.

Her phone rang at that precise moment and she lurched back, heart pounding. Somewhere deep inside, she half expected to see Paul's name pop up on her screen. But as she peered down, she saw it was Max.

She took a second to calm her nerves and then answered. "Hey, Max."

She knew she sounded strained, but there was nothing to be done for it. Her nerves were shot and she was holding on to her sanity by the thinnest of threads.

"Hey, Aunt Steph. You okay?"

"I'm…fine, yeah. Just going through the pile of Uncle Paul's call logs now."

"Actually, that's why I was calling," Max replied gently. "The bookstore is closed for the evening, and I wondered if you wanted some help. It can't be easy doing that alone. I could come by to split up the pile…or just for some moral support, if you want? I can stop by the shop and grab us each a cupcake on the way."

Stephanie gripped the phone tighter and wet her lips. "I would love that, but actually, I...I think I may have found a couple of potential leads for you to check into already."

There was silence on the other end of the phone, followed by a low hum. "Interesting. Like what?"

Stephanie shoved back a rush of guilt as she told Max about the early a.m. call from Lydia. She could hardly blame Max for wanting Paul to be what he'd always seemed like on the outside. Max, along with Gabe, and Stephanie and Paul's own kids, had idolized him. He was the one who snuck them candy when they weren't supposed to have it, let them stay up late, and added chocolate chips to their pancakes. He was fun and loving and supportive.

And, apparently, secretive. Now that they'd involved Max, it was too late to close that barn door. She wouldn't just forget about all of this, so Stephanie had to resign herself to her niece being part of this to the end.

Whether it turned out to be bitter, sweet, or a little bit of both.

Still, she couldn't bring herself to mention the other calls. Not yet. Not until she did some research, sat down and had a good, hard think about what it all meant.

"So do you think you can maybe give Lydia a call and see if she'd be willing to speak with you? I would do it myself, but—"

"Nope, we already decided, remember? If we want information, and we do, it's going to be easier if I ask the questions."

"I think Bryan has already clued her in, somewhat," Stephanie added. "He was going to ask around the office to see if anyone had gotten wind of a mistress or the like, so I imagine he spoke to Lydia. Just let her know that we aren't trying to besmirch his memory. There are just some unanswered questions that need to be resolved."

"I'll be very discreet," Max promised.

"They had a very good working relationship, and I know they were fond of one another. If she feels like he's being attacked, she might clam up out of loyalty."

"Roger that," Max replied. "Text me her phone number and I'll give her a call. I'm going to see if she will agree to meet me for a drink. I think if I explain it all in person, she'll be more likely to open up to me."

They finished their conversation and Stephanie disconnected. She went and brewed herself a pot of tea before shooting Max a text with Lydia's information. Just as she hit send, her phone trilled again and she lifted it to her ear.

"Sorry, Max, I just sent the number over. I just wanted to put on the kettle."

"Actually, this is Ethan...ah, Detective Jenkins. Is this Stephanie?"

Stephanie drew back in surprise. She hadn't expected to hear from him for another couple of days. "Hello, Detective. Sorry, I thought you were my niece calling me back."

"How are you holding up?"

She lifted her glasses and rubbed at her tired eyes before replying. "I'm...okay. It's been a really strange week." Inexplicably, she found herself opening up to him. She told him about the Lucy and Ethel routine at Paul's job, and about Max and her idea. She even told him about the calls to Paul's cell phone in the days following his death. It was only then that he stopped her babbling.

"That's odd. Are you sure he would've had his phone with him on the boat?" he asked in that low, soothing baritone.

"He never went anywhere without it. Especially not on the boat alone. I guess he could've dropped it or lost it on the way somewhere. Or maybe . . ." She trailed off, not wanting to say the words, but forcing them out anyway. "Maybe he knew he wasn't coming back and left it behind on purpose…so he couldn't be tracked."

The thought floored her, but Ethan cut in quickly. "If he planned this and was hoping to be presumed dead, he definitely would've taken the phone with him. He'd have wanted everything to seem normal. You told me that him having his phone was the norm, right?"

"Y-yes," she admitted, grateful for his level head right now. "Definitely."

"So it doesn't make sense for him to leave it behind on purpose if he was trying not to arouse suspicion. That means that he either lost the phone at some point prior, or there is some sort of mix-up at the phone company. Tell you what. I'm going to see if I can't make some calls and get to the bottom of this. I can't promise anything. Paul's death was ruled an accident, and without a court order, it's unlikely I'll get the phone company to give me detailed information, but I can at least talk to our guys here in tech and see if it's possible that his phone was registering calls after it was submerged. I'll give you a call back as soon as I know anything."

"Thanks a lot, Detective."

"Please, call me Ethan. And Stephanie?"

"Yes?" she asked, her throat feeling raw and achy. God, she hated that this stranger had been exposed to her at her most vulnerable, over and over.

"You're going to be all right. I know it might not seem like it right now. But one day, you're going to wake up, and it's going to hurt just a little less. I promise."

He disconnected and she stared at the phone for a long moment, letting his words sink in.

He sounded like he knew from experience. All she could do was hope that he was right. Because it had been almost three years now, and so far she felt as broken and messed up as she had the day Paul had died. Maybe even more so now, as she was forced to question their whole life together.

She sipped at her tea and picked up her phone, thumbing through the screen until she reached her collection of photos. Heart heavy, she flicked open an album she'd labeled "Ski bunnies." The first image that opened was of her and Paul at the top of Mount Mistletoe. They'd stopped off at the little ski lodge at the top for some food before their fifth run down. She wore a white ski jacket and was pink-cheeked and grinning as she cupped a steaming bowl of chowder. His dimples flashed like twin beacons of joy, his face pressed against hers as he held up a bread bowl heaping with beef stew.

Was that the face of the man she knew and loved, or that of a world class con man? Something told her the truth was close and getting closer every day.

The only question now was, would she be able to survive the fallout once it was revealed?

Chapter Eleven

Max called Lydia as soon as she got off the phone with her aunt, deciding the sooner they got answers, the better. She had the perfect excuse to get her uncle's assistant to meet her.

"Hi, Lydia," Max said, keeping her voice light. "I'm Max Burrows—Paul Ketterman's niece. I'm not sure if you'd heard, but his daughter Sarah is getting married in a few months."

"I *had* heard," she said, her voice breaking. "I got an invitation. I'm sure it must be difficult with Paul being gone."

"It is," Max admitted, "which is why I'm talking to people who knew Paul. We're putting together a presentation for the reception. I'd love to talk to you since you worked with him for so long. Could we maybe meet for coffee tonight?" When the woman hesitated, Max added, "I confess that I've been procrastinating and now I'm under a time crunch. So sorry for the late notice."

Lydia chuckled. "Oh, my dear, I don't have any plans, and I'd rather talk to you tonight than at lunch where I'm watching the clock. But I hate to drink coffee this late, so how do you feel about meeting at Petey's instead?"

Max blinked in surprise. Petey's was a local bar on the south side of town. She'd never been there because they catered to an older crowd. "Yeah, sure. What time?"

"I just need to feed my cat. Then I can head out the door."

"Okay, then," Max said, rushing over to her purse on the kitchen table. "I'll meet you there." Then she quickly added, "I'm brunette, and wearing a dark blue shirt and jeans."

The woman laughed. "No worries, dear. I'll be able to spot you."

Max hung up and hurried out the door, sorting through the ways to go about interviewing Lydia. The wedding angle was good to get Paul's assistant to a face-to-face meeting, but it didn't segue well into "do you know why Uncle Paul's cell phone was missing calls at the bottom of the ocean?" Max was open to a lot of possibilities, but the lost city of Atlantis having cell phone coverage wasn't one of them.

The parking lot was more than half full, which Max found surprising for a weekday night, but as soon as she walked in, she realized why. A band was playing on the small stage, and most of the patrons were on the dance floor in the middle of a line dance.

Max smiled to herself as she scanned the room, searching for someone who might be Lydia, then realized she'd never asked the other woman what she would be wearing. She headed to the bar, and a young man who looked familiar made his way over.

"Looking for your sugar daddy?" he teased with a wink. Leaning his forearm on the counter, his grin lit up his eyes.

"You always appeared to be too independent for that in high school."

Her mouth parted in surprise. "Tyler? Tyler Martin?" A smile spread across her face. "What are you doing here? Last I heard, you were in Portland."

"Gave up the rat race and came back home. My dad's Petey. He owns the place. He's about to retire, and I'll be taking over."

"I did the same. Gave up my job in Portland and came home," she said. "Although I started my own business at the same time as my mother."

He gave her an appreciative grin. "I know. I've actually driven past the bookstore a few times."

"You knew I was back in town and didn't call me? I haven't seen you at any First Fridays or anything else the younger crowd usually goes to around here."

He laughed. "That's because I'm always working here." He gestured to the dance floor. "It's a happenin' place."

She laughed too. "So I see. Maybe I should start hanging around here more often."

He tilted his head, still grinning. "I wouldn't be opposed to that, although the older guys will be swarming you like a bear to honey."

Her face flushed. Was he flirting? She'd had a crush on him in high school, but while he'd been in her circle of friends, he'd never seemed interested in her romantically.

"Does that mean I need to learn how to line dance?" she teased.

"I'll let you off the hook," he said, "as long as you hang out at the bar and talk to me."

Her stomach fluttered. Tyler had always been one of the cuter boys in school, but he'd grown into a handsome man.

"I was actually considering calling you," he said, turning serious.

"Oh?"

"I have a business idea, and I was wanting to get your input."

"Oh." Talk about a disappointment. "Shoot."

He glanced around, then leaned closer. "Have you considered adding a bar to your bookstore?"

"What?"

He lifted a hand. "Now hear me out. I'm not trying to tell you how to run your bookstore, and feel free to shoot me down. If you add a bar—with a heavy focus on wine— you could draw patrons who would be there to drink, but also buy books."

She narrowed her eyes. "Are you suggesting my bookstore isn't good enough?" The fact that he was so blunt about it hurt, but the fact was that it wasn't. She had yet to make a profit, even after adding a coffee bar that served pastries from her mother's cupcake shop. Business had increased, but it hadn't been enough, and if things didn't turn around soon, she'd be out of business by the end of the year...if not sooner.

His eyes flew wide in horror. "What? No! I just had this idea and I can't do it myself...what with running the bar for my dad. But you already have a bookstore, and I thought maybe we could be partners in the bar part—I supply the booze and wine—I can even come in and teach classes on wine. I became a sommelier and now it's just going to waste."

"You became a sommelier?" she asked in surprise.

He lifted a shoulder into a half shrug. "My brother was supposed to take over the bar, and I was going to open my own restaurant. But fate had other plans."

Max cringed, suddenly remembering some of her friends telling her about Graham Martin's car accident and subsequent death days later. But she'd been in the middle of her own crisis and it had fallen off her radar. She felt like crap for not offering her condolences the second she saw him. "Tyler, I'm so sorry."

His mouth flattened into a thin line before he said, "It is what it is. Graham's a hard act to follow." A grin spread across his face, but it looked forced. "But now I'm back and desperate to use some of my expertise. Books and wine seemed like a natural fit, but forgive me for insinuating that you should just jump on board with my plan. I've considered approaching you for months but have been too chicken to pull the trigger."

"Because you expected me to take it badly?" I asked, cringing as she realized she *had*.

He hesitated, then said, "No, because you're a beautiful woman, Max Burrows, and I've had a crush on you since high school. I wasn't sure it was a good idea to mix business with someone I'm so interested in."

Max couldn't have been more surprised than if a cow had walked in playing an accordion. "Tyler . . ."

"Excuse me," said a woman to Max's right. "Max?"

Max gave Tyler an astonished look, then reluctantly turned toward the reason she was here. "Lydia?" She plastered on a smile, letting the woman know she was happy to see her—which was true. She just had *terrible* timing. Holding out her hand, she said, "Thank you so much for meeting me."

The woman ignored her hand and wrapped her beefy arms around Max, squeezing her in a tight hug. "I'm a hugger."

"Me too," Max said, although usually not with absolute strangers.

Lydia released her and motioned to a back corner. "It'll be quieter back there, but let's order our drinks first."

She turned to the bar and waved Tyler back over. "Hey, Ty. I'll have my usual and my friend here will have…?"

Lydia gave Max an inquisitive look.

"Red wine," Max said, meeting Tyler's gaze. "Nothing too dry. I'll let you pick."

Tyler's face lit up. "I'll bring them right over to your table."

Lydia glanced between Max and the bartender, then headed to a table in a dark corner. "I take it you know Tyler?"

"We went to high school together."

"He's a good son. Up and left his job at a big restaurant in Portland and moved home to take over Petey's bar. Graham had been running it, because Petey's in such bad health." They sat down and Lydia leaned closer. "Ty's a good man." Then she winked.

Max laughed. "Are you playing matchmaker?"

"Perhaps. I just know truly good men are hard to find," Lydia said, turning sober.

A fact Max knew all too well. Most men she'd dated had turned out to be more interested in their own lives than building a relationship with her. Her own father had cheated on her mother. That was why she'd found it so hard to believe that Uncle Paul would cheat on Aunt Steph. Most little girls idealized their fathers, but Max had idealized her uncle. She'd taken his death nearly as hard as her cousins, and she couldn't bear the thought that he'd been less of a man than she'd known him to be.

"Uncle Paul was a good man," she said before she could stop herself, but she felt the need to affirm it verbally, as though to publicly announce her belief.

Lydia nodded, lowering her gaze. "One of the best."

"Do you have any stories about Uncle Paul we might be able to use for the presentation?" Max asked. Despite her purpose for being there, she realized she was hungry to hear them.

"Do I have stories?" Lydia laughed. "How much time do you have?"

Max cast a glance to Tyler, who was heading toward them with their drinks, and a smile spread across her face. "As much time as we need."

Tyler approached them and said, "Excuse the intrusion, ladies. Lydia, here's your Sex on the Beach."

"Don't I wish!" Lydia said with a laugh.

Tyler shot her a grin, then placed a wine glass in front of Max. "I chose a two-year-old merlot."

Then he told her the name and the location of the winery.

She laughed when she realized it was a wine found on most restaurant menus.

He gave her an apologetic look. "It's the best we have here, but maybe I could take you out to dinner at Pierre's in Pickford and show you my real expertise."

Max had gone to Pierre's last December with her then-boyfriend, Robbie, but she'd never made it through the front door, instead dumping him on the spot when he'd struck her. It wasn't a place that held warm and fuzzy memories, and something deep down told her that a date with Tyler would be special. Not something to taint with bad memories. "You've got a deal on one condition," she said. "We can't eat at Pierre's." Surprise filled his eyes, so she added, "When

I tell you the reason why, you'll know you've earned my trust. Until that time, I hope you'll respect my reasons and suggest somewhere else."

He nodded, his eyes lighting up. "How about I surprise you?"

The butterflies were back. Was she seriously setting up a date while pumping Uncle Paul's assistant for information? Aunt Anna would be so pleased. "You've got a deal. When did you have in mind?"

"I'm off on Monday nights. How about I pick you up at your apartment? You tell me what time is convenient."

"Seven," she said, suddenly self-conscious that Lydia was glued to every word.

Tyler looked elated, and that was when Max knew he was different than any other man she'd dated. Tyler wouldn't be afraid to show her how he really felt.

"I feel like I'll need to speak at your wedding," Lydia said softly as Tyler headed back to the bar. She smiled before picking up her drink and taking a sip. "I'll be able to tell the tale of how you first met."

Max didn't correct her, and something warmed inside of her at the mention of their wedding. While Max wasn't in a hurry to get married, she would like to meet "the one." The man who loved her with all his being. Her best friend.

Her own Uncle Paul.

A topic she needed to get back to. "About Uncle Paul . . ."

Lydia chuckled knowingly. "What do you want to hear? What a thoughtful man he was? How he liked to play Secret Santa to the employees in need around the holidays? How he bought coffee and food for the few homeless in Bluebird Bay so often that they knew him by name and arranged to go to his funeral? Or how he sponsored countless basketball, softball, and Little League teams?" Tears filled her eyes. "There are so many stories."

"I want to hear them all," Max said with a lump in her throat. Her grief was resurfacing and she wasn't sure how to handle it.

Lydia grabbed a tissue from her purse and dabbed her eyes. "We'd be here for days, so I'll just tell you the highlights." Then she spent the next forty-five minutes telling Max story after story about the good things Paul had done for others, only confirming he was the man Max had been led to believe her whole life.

They were silent for a few seconds before Max looked into Lydia's eyes. This trip down memory lane and the opportunity to see her beloved uncle through the eyes of someone else who clearly loved him had been a gift. But it was time to get down to the nitty-gritty. "Do you know if Uncle Paul routinely met clients outside the office?"

Lydia shook her head. "No. He was pretty adamant about keeping business in the office. Always said he would never be one of those guys who lived to work, and drawing those lines was important to him. He really enjoyed his hobbies and your aunt Stephanie's and the kids' company so much. That time was sacred to him. I think he was afraid once he left the door open even a crack, his two worlds would collide and he'd wind up taking work home with him and the like. He never wanted to do that."

Max's heart sank. "So it seems unlikely that he would have met a client for a business meal shortly before his death?"

Lydia's face paled as she nodded. "Unlikely, yes. Why do you ask, dear?"

No. No. Max refused to let her thoughts go there. "Do you know if Uncle Paul was acting strangely or had any clients that were different than the usual?"

Lydia started to say something, then stopped.

"It's okay," Max encouraged. "I know he was a great person. This is just about getting answers to some lingering questions. That's all."

"There was a woman...," Lydia murmured, trailing off.

Max placed her hand over Lydia's. "I think Uncle Paul was involved in something," she said, going with the uneasy feeling that had been brewing in her gut since talking to Aunt Steph. "I know he met someone the morning of his death. A woman."

A fire lit up Lydia's eyes. "Paul Ketterman would sooner cut off his right hand than cheat on his wife. Those two were the definition of love, and I won't hear of anything else."

Relief washed through Max and the muscles in her back relaxed. "I don't think he was either, but some things aren't adding up, and we're trying to sort out what it means." She paused, then said, "Aunt Steph can't bring herself to move on until we get to the bottom of it all."

"What do you mean?"

Max twisted her mouth to the side. "All we know for sure is that he met with this woman. It's not much to go on, but I'm hoping that whatever you can tell me will be helpful in locating her. Can you tell me about the woman you mentioned?"

Lydia hesitated and then began talking in a low voice. "A couple of months before Paul's death, a woman called the office. She refused to give her name, but she insisted on talking to Paul. She sounded desperate. Paul took the call and about ten minutes later, he walked out of his office and told me he was leaving and didn't know when he'd be back. He didn't return for two hours, and then he told me to hold all his calls. He shut his door and didn't come out until after I left for the day."

"Do you have any idea what it was about?"

"Not a clue," Lydia said, pursing her lips and shaking her head. "Nothing like that had ever happened before."

"Did anything like it happen after?"

"No, but I'm sure I saw him with her after that."

"Where?"

"Paul Ketterman is a good man," Lydia said insistently.

"No one believes that more strongly than me, Lydia. Anything you tell me will help."

Lydia nodded, pursing her lips. After several seconds, she glanced down at her empty glass and said, "I saw them sitting together at the park. It was a nice day and I decided to take my lunch there. I thought Paul must have had the same idea, but then I saw he wasn't eating. He and the blonde woman were deep in conversation, so I didn't say anything."

"Did he look happy? Sad?" Max prompted.

"He looked serious. Worried. They weren't holding hands or touching in any way," Lydia said. "They weren't having an affair."

"How long before the accident did you see them?"

"A couple of months."

"Do you know how long they were there?"

"I didn't sit near them, but when I was throwing out my trash, they were still there. So at least half an hour. They looked like they were having a bit of an argument or disagreement at the end. Then she got up and got in her car and left."

"Do you know what kind of car she drove?"

Max's pulse raced as the older woman nodded.

"Yup. I'll never forget it. An old yellow Ford Mustang. My son had one. I'd guess a 1976 or '77. Maine plates."

"Thank you, Lydia," Max said, patting the woman's hand again. "You've been more helpful than you know."

"I hope you and Stephanie find the answers you need," Lydia said. "And that you find a way to put the whole thing to rest."

That was Max's hope too...but they were just getting started.

Chapter Twelve

B ut *again*, she said that there was no way Paul would've been having an affair," Max repeated for the third time in as many minutes.

"She cared about him," Stephanie replied dully, pushing the cupcake on her plate around listlessly. "They worked together for decades. People turn a blind eye to faults when they love someone."

Who would know better than her, after all? She'd apparently been doing it for decades.

Cee-cee squeezed the bridge of her nose between her thumb and forefinger and sighed. "The thing is, it's not just Lydia saying that. Everyone is saying the same thing. We can't ignore that, Stephanie," she chided, untying her apron and laying it on the little bistro table between them. "Guys with weak character don't hide it all that well for long...Once it's out in the open and someone says it out loud, generally speaking, people are quick to confirm it. When people found out about Nate, not a single person was shocked. Angry? Yes. Baffled? Some. But shocked?" She shrugged. "Not really." She blanched and turned to Max, patting her hand. "Sorry, honey. Not to speak ill of your dad."

"You're just calling a spade a spade, Mom," Max said with a shrug. "I'm an adult. I know what he is and what he's done. I just hope he can grow from those mistakes. I know right about now, he's having some major regrets. Mandy is apparently a living nightmare, and so is her silly little dog. Dad can't get a moment of peace in the house with the two of them. He doesn't want to admit he was wrong and threw his life away over nothing, but it's getting to breaking point. I give it until the end of summer before he tucks his tail between his legs and walks. He's not one to endure any level of personal suffering for long if he has a choice."

"Whatever the case, it's water under the bridge, and he did me a favor," Cee-cee said with a nod. "I'm happier than I've ever been. Anna's done with her radiation and chemo, Pop finally gave in on the whole living arrangement thing. Now, if we can just get to the bottom of this thing with Paul, maybe . . ."

"I can start to move on too?" Stephanie asked, staring out at the waves as she forked up another bite of Chocolate Sin cupcake and shoveled it into her mouth with a sigh.

She'd been wrestling with the ramifications of Max and Lydia's talk since the night before, and was still in a state of semi-shock. Once could've been passed off as a coincidence. Maybe. But two secret meetings with a strange woman no one recognized, including his trusted assistant? What else could she be but a mistress? Especially if they'd argued...

"Even criminal courts take into account character witnesses. And Paul has gobs of them. I just don't know," Cee-cee muttered, her brows knitting in confusion. "One minute, my brain tells me if it walks like a duck and talks like a duck, it's a duck and Paul was cheating. The next, my heart tells me something else. I don't think you can accept evidence of a second meeting with this woman as confirmation that he was having an affair. As much as I hate to admit it, I think you need to press on and find out for sure now. None of us will rest until you do."

Stephanie was glad to have her sister's support, but the very idea of resting was so foreign to her, it was almost laughable. When was the last time she'd had a decent night's sleep? She couldn't even recall. And when she did manage to string a few hours together, her rest was highlighted by nightmares of her husband under water, flailing as he gasped for air.

She said a silent prayer for the millionth time that he didn't suffer. No matter what he'd done in his life, no one deserved to die like he had.

If he's even dead at all.

She shoved the all-too confusing thought from her mind and finished the last of her cupcake before pushing away from the table.

"Max, I really appreciate you talking to Lydia for me. I think I need a couple of days to let this all sink in and decide what my next move should be. Todd starts at the clinic tomorrow, and it's going to be a busy few days trying to get him acclimated, but I plan to take the whole weekend off and hopefully make some progress on finding out who this woman is."

She was keeping it intentionally vague, not wanting to share too much info about Ethan's role in this all. He was already going out on a limb for her by calling in favors for her. The last thing she wanted was for him to get into trouble for trying to be a nice guy.

"Okay, but remember what we talked about, Aunt Stephanie. Keep an open mind to all the possibilities instead of looking for proof that Uncle Paul was cheating," Max reminded her gently. "He saw this woman at the park...Do you think he'd have done it somewhere so public if he couldn't explain their connection? People who cheat skulk around and meet in motels, not at public parks."

Her niece had a point, but going down that road was just as dangerous. "If we're keeping our minds open, part of that means being open to the possibility that Paul was a great uncle, a great co-worker, and a nice guy...who may have gotten his head turned by a pretty blonde. So let's put a pin in this for now, until we know more, all right?"

Max bit her lip and nodded as Cee-cee stood and walked Stephanie to the shop door. She paused and grabbed the white bakery box sitting on the checkout counter.

"Two creamsicle, and two passion fruit and white chocolate, Pop's favorite. Tell him a couple customers were asking for him today."

Stephanie took the box and winced. "If I tell him that, he's going to start grilling me about when he can come back. I just don't know if it's a good idea."

Their father had passed out samples and greeted customers at the cupcake shop a couple days a week until the weather had grown bitter cold. Cee-cee had indicated she wanted to have him start back up in the spring, but his moods were so dicey, Steph had hesitated at first, worried he might offend some of the customers or start an argument. Not to mention the last thing she wanted was for Cee-cee to put her business at risk. But Cee-cee had insisted all would be fine if he started back to work And there was no doubt it meant a lot to their dad to feel needed. Coming to the shop and helping gave him a purpose.

"I think he'll be all right. And if he's not, I think people will understand and be very forgiving if I explain. The benefits outweigh the risks to me, so as long as he's feeling well, he can start back next week."

Steph eyed her dubiously. "He's awfully cranky, but if you're sure . . ."

"I am," Cee-cee replied. "Now go on," she added, peering out the door at the ominous, graying sky. "Before you get caught in the rain."

"Talk to you later," Stephanie said as she pushed out into the cool air. She tugged her windbreaker tighter around her shoulders and shivered. Spring in Northern Maine could mean seventy degrees on a good day or thirty on a bad one. This evening, it was halfway between the two, and getting wet on top of it would only add to the chill factor. She quickened her pace to a slow jog as the first drops of rain pelted her face.

She'd just gotten into her SUV and set down the cupcake box on the seat beside her when her cell phone chimed.

It was a text from Ethan.

At Mo's Diner eating dinner and just got some info for you. Got a few minutes to talk?

A shiver went through her as she stared down at the text. Did he have news for her about Paul's blonde friend as well? She almost wanted to ignore the message. Her mental and emotional cup had runneth over for the day and she was bone-tired. It was only the flicker of Ethan's kind, understanding face in her mind that made her type back.

On my way.

If he did have more bad news for her, at least she'd hear it in a familiar environment and from someone she was starting to consider a friend. Besides, she could also get out of cooking dinner if she snagged a quart of Mo's famous chowder while she was there.

Two birds, one stone.

That decided, she buckled up and made the short drive over. By the time she got to Mo's and found Ethan, his food was being delivered. A full pot roast dinner. She smiled at the waitress and slid into the booth across from him.

"Can I get you something to eat?" the waitress asked with a pleasant grin.

"Actually, I just stuffed my face with a big, fat cupcake, but I will take a cup of tea for here and a quart of the New England clam chowder to go, please."

The waitress jotted down her order and then melted away as Stephanie faced a solemn-looking Ethan.

"You look like you've been through a war," he observed, getting straight to the heart of the matter. She probably should be offended, but in truth, she liked that about him. No dancing around the uncomfortable stuff. She met his candor with no less.

"I feel like it too. It's been a rough go lately, and I suspect it's only going to get rougher. Do I have that right?" she asked with a rueful shake of her head, gesturing for him to start on his food. "No sense in letting it get cold. Eat and talk."

He stuck his fork into a roasted potato and paused. "There's no easy way to say this, so I'm just going to say it plain. I spoke to my guys in tech. There is no way Paul's phone could've registered those missed calls if it was destroyed in the water."

The news wasn't much of a surprise. Everything she'd read online had supported that theory. Still, she found herself shaken by the potential ramifications of the news. She was still trying to wrap her head around it when Ethan continued.

"You should also know that I checked into the phone number the calls came from in the days following the accident." He set his fork down with a clatter and leaned closer, his voice dropping to a murmur. "The calls came from what we call a burner phone. It's not a number registered to a specific customer or phone contract. It's the type of device—"

"That married men and women use when they're cheating," she cut in with a nod, grateful when the waitress returned and set her steaming mug of tea on the table between them. She thanked her and took a bracing sip before locking gazes with Ethan again. "It really does seem as if all the clues are pointing in the same direction, doesn't it?"

He didn't reply to that, picking his fork up and taking a bite of his dinner. Her mind whirred like a top spinning out of control as she tried to decide what to do next.

"The burner was last used in Boston to make those exact calls, and has had no activity since. It's my guess that it's been destroyed," Ethan continued when he was done chewing. "Short of dredging this all up again and reopening an investigation into Paul's death—which I don't think we have enough cause from a procedural standpoint to do at this point—we're at a bit of a dead end here. I'm sorry. I'm sure none of this is what you wanted to hear."

"There's more, actually," Stephanie admitted, cupping her tea mug and letting the warmth seep into her icy hands. "My niece spoke to Paul's former assistant. She'd seen the blonde as well. Saw her and Paul at the park shortly before his death. It looked like they were exchanging some cross words and she took off in an old yellow Ford Mustang, '76 or '77, with Maine plates."

Ethan's eyes narrowed. "Cross words? As in a lover's quarrel?"

The very thought made Stephanie physically ill, but she pressed on. "She couldn't say. Lydia idolized Paul, so she stopped short of calling it that. But what else could it have been?"

Ethan swiped his firm mouth with his napkin and set down his utensils again, pinning her with his all-too perceptive gaze. "This is important, Stephanie, so consider your answer carefully, all right?"

She nodded and swallowed hard.

"Do you believe, in your heart of hearts, that Paul could be alive out there somewhere?"

That very question had been tugging at the edge of her consciousness ever since she'd found out about his meeting with this woman the morning of his death. Now, she faced it head-on and let all the emotions that came along with it roll through her. She found herself choking back tears when she finally replied.

"No."

"Because?" Ethan pressed gently.

"Because I knew it...I felt it." She'd never said the words aloud, because they sounded crazy, even to herself. She was a woman of science. And, still... "When the police called and told me the wreckage of the boat had been found, I already knew he was gone. I can't explain it, but it was sort of like this thick sense of dread in my heart. A light went out that day, and it's never come back on. I truly believe he's gone."

To her surprise, Ethan didn't even blink. "Then the only questions that remain are who this woman was, what she was to him, and where his phone went on the day of the accident. I can't promise anything, but I might be able to make some headway on the first piece of that puzzle by contacting a friend at the DMV. Maybe if we do that, we can figure out the rest. But you need to be prepared for the fact that you might never know, Stephanie. And that's a hard pill to swallow. One that might require some help."

He reached into his jacket pocket and tugged out a business card.

"Doctor Yang is someone we use on the force. She helps with grief, PTSD, and all sorts of issues that come up in my line of work. Maybe talking to her can help you grapple with some of this."

Stephanie took the card with a nod.

He wasn't the first person who'd suggested she needed therapy of some kind, but he was the straw that broke the camel's back. She was sick of fighting it. She'd always thought she was so strong…too strong to need help.

It was time to face the fact that she was wrong.

"I'll call her first thing tomorrow."

The waitress brought over her to-go container of soup, and she made to hand over her credit card, but Ethan stopped her.

"This one's on me. I'll call you when I know something," he said, his tone brooking no argument.

She thanked him and snatched up her bag, on the brink of tears.

She'd thought losing Paul had been the worst day of her life. That she'd never feel pain like that again. But it seemed like pain had pulled up a chair two years ago and settled in for the long haul.

How much more could she take?

Chapter Thirteen

"Peekaboo! I see you!" Anna cooed, chuckling as Teddy let out a squeal of delight. God, was there anything sweeter than a baby's laugh?

Beckett's grandson had been an unexpected bonus in their relationship. One she hadn't even considered until a few months into their dating. In fact, before Teddy, she might have even considered grandkids to be a detriment. But as time passed, she'd come to look forward to the days Beckett was asked to babysit. All she had to do was stick out her tongue and blow raspberries, and he thought she was hilarious. He loved her cooking, which was saying something because her lack of prowess in the kitchen was known far and wide. But pastina with butter and peas was easy enough to make, even for her.

Beckett came sailing into the room from the kitchen holding two steaming mugs of coffee, one ceramic, one to-go cup.

"I just got a call from a guy who is stuck on Monterey and blocking traffic. I'd pass it along, but he's a nervous wreck and people are beeping at him like crazy . . ."

He handed her the ceramic cup and winced.

"You think it would be okay if I give him a quick tow? Take me an hour, tops."

Anna blinked at him, shot a glance at Teddy, who flashed his signature single-toothed smile, and then back at Beckett, panic curling around her.

"And, like, leave me here alone with Teddy?" she squeaked.

Beckett held up a hand and chuckled. "Forget it. No problem. I can call Pat up in Winston. It will take him a while to get down here, but it's not an emergency."

"Nope." Anna stood and wiped her sweaty palms on the thighs of her jeans. "That's ridiculous. You go ahead and do your job. I'm just being a chicken. How hard can it be to watch over one sweet little angel for an hour or two? So long as you think Austin and Melinda wouldn't mind?"

Over the last few months, she'd formed an easy friendship with Beckett's son and his wife, but chatting over dinner and trusting someone with your precious baby were two very different things...

"They love you. Not only that, they trust you and think you're so good with Teddy. If it makes you feel better, I'll text Austin and let him know you're in charge while I'm gone."

Anna sucked in a deep breath and nodded, turning her gaze onto a still-grinning Teddy. "Sounds good. We're going to have so much fun, aren't we, little buddy?"

Beckett swiped his keys off the dining table before bending low to kiss her forehead.

"You got this, kiddo."

She let out a snort. "Of course I do. It's going to be great."

He leaned in to kiss Teddy and laid a smooch on one plump cheek and then headed for the door.

"I'll put his car seat in the back of yours on my way out in case you want to go somewhere. And I'll call before I come home to see what you want to eat. We can use the cash from this tow to pick up a great bottle of wine and some Italian from Monzano's."

The promise of fettuccini Alfredo with chicken and broccoli followed by a fat slice of boozy tiramisu had her shaking off the last of her nerves.

"Love you," he called over his shoulder a second before the door closed.

Anna stared at the spot he'd just vacated for long moments after he left.

Love you.

They'd said the words to one another before. Him first. It had taken her a while longer. Not because she didn't feel it. More because she did and it terrified her. Now it was something they tossed back and forth easily. Like a longtime couple. And she had to admit…she didn't hate it.

"Brrrrppptthp," Teddy said, banging his hands on his high chair tray as he gleefully formed bubbles with his mouth.

"You want me to bust you out of jail?" Anna asked with a smile as she stood and set her coffee down, making sure it was far enough away from busy little hands.

She was really getting the hang of this whole having a baby around thing.

"What do you think we should do, Teddy? Want to play with your blocks?"

She unfastened the straps and pulled out the tray before hoisting a squirmy Teddy from the high chair. On impulse, she gave him a quick squeeze, which he returned happily.

This was…nice. And so domestic of her. Gone were the days of last-minute trips to the Congo to take pictures of apes. She'd expected to miss it. So far, though, her life felt too full to miss traveling. Her work at the conservation center fueled her creatively, and her relationship with Beckett fulfilled her emotionally. Not to mention having her sisters and father close. Maybe she was still high on the fact that she was cancer-free.

Not that every day was rainbows and lollipops. She'd gone through grueling rounds of treatment, as well as a double mastectomy in order to lower her chances of the cancer returning. And while she felt healthy, it had been a blow to her confidence seeing what the insidious disease had done to her body. Some days, it took work to love herself and not let her scars and the changes define her. It definitely helped that Beckett didn't have to work on it at all. He loved her, head to toe, before and after her procedures, and he made sure to show it.

She let out a happy sigh as she set Teddy on the hardwood floor. He was still for exactly a nanosecond before his little legs starting churning and he motored off toward the toy box Beckett had made him last Christmas.

She laughed and jogged behind him, hot on his tail. For the next half hour, they played together. She read from a soft, squishy book filled with colorful images of animals that made sounds when you pressed them. Teddy tried to fit square blocks into star-shaped holes. The two of them lay on their bellies and then rolled across the floor. It was all so easy.

Too easy.

So when the smell of something so foul her eyes began to water filled the room, for a second, she wasn't sure what it was. A suspicious glance at Teddy's grinning face helped her fill in the blanks and she groaned.

"Aw, buddy. My only hope is that this smells worse than it is."

But the diaper gods were against her, because when she carried Teddy down the hall to his changing table and unsnapped his pants to check the damage, she nearly fainted. It was a critical blowout. The kind that haunted a person for weeks to come. Down his legs, up his back. He looked like he'd been lying in brown paint.

She realized with a wince that she'd probably unwittingly contributed to the carnage by rolling around on the floor with him.

Anna plugged her nose and gave herself a quick pep talk.

"No biggie. Just a little poop. Nothing to see here. A little wipie action, a fresh diaper, maybe some lotion, and we're back on track, Teddy my boy."

But Teddy was already beginning to squirm. Anna reached over and plucked a stuffed bear from the shelf overhead and handed it to the baby. Then she went to work. It wasn't easy. More than once, she had to lay a staying hand on Teddy's round little belly, turn away and take a breath of fresh, untainted air. But soon enough, she'd gotten him all cleaned up and dressed in fresh clothes and slathered her hands with hand sanitizer.

"We did it!" she cheered.

Teddy tugged the arm of the little bear from his mouth and cheered with her. It was only then that she realized the stuffed animal was winking at her.

She narrowed her gaze and gently pried the bear from Teddy's fingers. One shiny black eye stared back at her. The other side was just a few pieces of tattered black thread.

She gaped at the bear, then at Teddy. Her heart hammered in her chest as she reached for the baby's hands, prying open his fingers in search of the missing piece of plastic.

Nada.

"Oh my God. Oh my God." Anna scooped up Teddy and then the bear, searching the changing table and floor furiously for the eye and coming up empty.

Teddy gurgled and she took the opportunity to try to peer into his mouth, but could see nothing.

He was breathing. That was the most important part. But that dang bear had two eyes not five minutes before. It was small enough that Teddy could've swallowed it and not choked, but that didn't mean he wasn't in danger.

She stood motionless, racking her brain for what to do. She likely couldn't take him to the doctor as she wasn't his parent, but she couldn't just sit here and worry...

She made a snap decision as she sprinted down the hallway, tucking the bear under her arm as she pried her cell phone from her pocket. She thumbed out a number, nearly swooning with relief when the call was connected.

"Hey, it's me. Keep an exam room open. I'm on my way there with Teddy."

Fifteen minutes later, she was pacing around a small white room breathing in the antiseptic smell of medicine as her sister let out a snick of mock disapproval.

"Just for the record, once again, you know I'm a veterinarian, not a pediatrician, right?"

"I get it. Har har. Anna is such an irresponsible babysitter that she nearly let her charge choke and then brought him to Dr. Doolittle for treatment. Hilarious stuff. Just tell me, is he going to be okay?"

Steph nodded, effortlessly lifting Teddy to rest on her hip. It looked so easy and comfortable for her. Why was it so hard for Anna?

"He's going to be fine. We can do an X-ray, but I truly don't think it's necessary. The eye is pretty small and doesn't have any sharp edges. These things almost always come out in the wash, so to speak. Tell his parents and Beckett what happened and to keep an eye out for it. That's my medical opinion."

Anna slumped with relief and then lowered herself into the plastic chair in the corner of the room.

"I don't even know how it happened. One second, it was all fine, the next, the eye was gone. Who would make a toy like this anyway?" she demanded, happy for a place to redirect her anger and guilt. "Talk about shoddy craftsmanship."

Steph was nodding, but her brow was furrowed as she studied Teddy and Anna knew she wasn't listening.

"Steph? Is everything okay?"

Please, God, don't let her have thought of some other reason this could harm Teddy.

"Yes, fine. I just had a thought." Steph laid Teddy on the papered table and then made quick work of unfastening the snaps of his sweatpants and unbuttoning his little shirt. As she tugged his onesie down, the unmistakable sound of plastic hitting the floor and rolling echoed through the silent room.

Anna let out a gasp, followed the sound, and found herself locking gazes with one shiny black eye.

"Holy crap!" Anna shouted as she bent to pick up the cause of all her woes. "It's here! He didn't swallow it."

A suspicious sound bubbled from Stephanie, and Anna wheeled on her, scowling at her giggling sister, wanting to strangle her for thinking any of this was funny.

"How is this funny?" she demanded. She wanted to stay irritated, but she was so happy, it didn't stick.

"Rule number one when it comes to babies: If they can eat it, they will. Rule number two: Make sure they ate it before you panic."

"Got it," Anna said sheepishly. "Oh, Teddy, Anna-Banana is so relieved you didn't eat the eye. Now Mommy and Daddy don't have to shield you from me."

"It wasn't your fault regardless, Anna. Just make sure to tell Beckett to get rid of that bear."

Anna turned and found the bear sitting on the countertop. She tossed it into the trash can and turned back to Teddy. "I'm gonna buy you a better bear. A polar bear! With eyes that don't pop off instead."

Teddy was too preoccupied with Steph's stethoscope to care, but Anna felt like the weight of the world had been lifted from her shoulders. She thanked her sister profusely and scooped up Teddy, ready to head back to Beckett's. She'd just made it to the door when it swung open and a familiar-looking man stepped in.

"Hey, Bryan. How are you?" Anna asked with a smile.

Paul's business partner conjured a quick grin for baby Teddy and nodded to Anna politely, but he looked pale and distressed. "I'm okay. Good to see you again, Anna. I actually came by to talk to Stephanie."

Anna glanced over her shoulder at her sister, who stood beside the reception desk, her welcoming smile turning into a worried frown. "Sure, of course, Bryan. Is everything all right?"

Bryan shot Anna a glance and then lowered his voice to a murmur. "Actually, I think it's best if we talk alone. I figured the clinic was closing soon and we might go for a walk so we can chat?"

Stephanie opened her mouth to reply and then faltered as she shot Anna a nervous glance.

"I've got to go anyway. Call me later, sis. Love you."

Anna made her way back to her car, her Teddy victory losing some of its shine under the weight of Bryan's concern.

He'd come by instead of calling first, and he looked like he was on his way to a funeral. Whatever he had to tell her sister was going to hurt. Anna just hoped that Stephanie could take yet another blow.

Chapter Fourteen

Stephanie pulled her cardigan more tightly around her shoulders as she and Bryan fell into step beside one another.

"I'm sorry I didn't call first," he began gently.

"No problem. I don't have much time, though. Todd is coming by the office this evening so we can go over the intake system and things. He starts working with me in just a few days, and there's a bit of a learning curve to it all."

She tried to act normal but could hear just how brittle her voice sounded. She had seen the tension in Bryan's face the second he'd stepped into the clinic. He wasn't here to deliver good news. And as much as she knew she should get it over with, she couldn't help but continue her babbling out of some misguided, instinctive sense of self-preservation.

"I'm so proud of him. Third in his class! Isn't that amazing? He's going to do really well here. I'm sure of it. Ever since he was little, he's always loved animals. Paul and I couldn't go a week without him bringing home an injured bird or orphaned baby bunny. He's got such a big heart—"

"Stephanie," Bryan murmured, slowing to a stop and laying a hand on her forearm.

She met his sympathetic gaze and the sadness in his eyes was almost her undoing. She looked away, focusing her attention on the tree line in the distance.

"Did you ever get more information on the blonde woman you were looking for?"

She considered his question and was about to answer but hesitated. On top of the information Max had gotten from Lydia, there was also the matter of the burner phone that Ethan had discovered and his confirmation that Paul's phone hadn't been with him on the boat that day. Not to mention the digging Ethan planned to do going forward. He'd made it very clear that he wasn't acting in an official capacity, and the last thing she wanted was to get him into trouble for helping her. Better to keep that part of things close to the vest until she could come up with a feasible explanation for the intel she'd been collecting. If and when there was something of substance to share, she'd make sure to tell Bryan. Right now, there was nothing but dead ends, guesses, and suppositions. On her end, at least...

"Not much. I do know that Paul met with this woman at least one other time, though. And that they had some sort of argument or falling-out. I still don't know who she is or what their connection is, but I have a couple irons in the fire to try to figure out her identity. I have some questions I feel like only she can answer."

Bryan grimaced and nodded, blowing out a long breath. "I was afraid you were going to say that."

"What do you mean?"

"Are you sure you really need to speak with her, Stephanie? You might not want to hear what she has to say. Maybe some things truly are better left alone . . ."

And here it came. The axe, about to fall. She dropped any pretense of being okay and gripped his forearm tightly.

"You yourself swore up and down Paul would never cheat," she whispered. "You said he loved me more than anything."

Bryan's Adam's apple worked even as the muscle in his jaw ticked.

"I still believe he did, Stephanie. But I did some checking and found something. Something I almost can't believe myself."

"Just say it," she managed, the breath sawing in and out of her lungs as she braced herself for impact.

"I did some checking into Paul's travel and business expense reports for the months leading up to his death. There were several…concerning, or at least confusing, charges." He scrubbed a hand down his face and let out a groan. "God, I'm so sorry to have to tell you this, Stephanie.

"One was for a hotel room. Three nights at the Radisson. He traveled on occasion and had charged rooms before, but this one was for a hotel just thirty minutes away, in Maplethorpe. Then, there was a second charge on that same date. I'm so sorry to tell you this, but it was to a flower delivery service. I had hopes that maybe it was a getaway for the two of you for an anniversary or something and he just used his business credit card in error. But when I looked back at his time off that month, he hadn't taken a single vacation day. He did, however, take half days during that time period."

Which meant he'd apparently gone to work like normal, raised no suspicions, and then left at lunchtime to spend a few hours cavorting with his mistress before coming home at night.

To her.

To their bed.

Her chest felt like it was going to cave in as she blinked back tears.

"I'm sorry to have to be the one to tell you all this, but I think we have our answers now." Bryan slipped a comforting arm around her shoulder and pulled her in close. "I know how hard this must be. Do you think with Todd coming in maybe you can take some time off? Give yourself a chance to come to terms with all of this? It's a lot, and as much as Paul always said you were Superwoman, news like this can break even the strongest of us."

"A...friend gave me the number of a therapist," she admitted, still reeling as she tried to align the image of her doting, loving husband with the image of this...other man. One who slunk around and paid for hotel rooms with other women.

"What shop did he use?" she demanded, the words catching in her throat.

Bryan pulled back, clearly confused. "What do you mean?"

"Which flower shop?"

She could see by his expression that he was taken aback by the seemingly inane question, but she didn't care. She needed to hear the answer.

"The Gilded Lily, I believe was the name. Why?"

"I wanted to know if it was the same place he used to send me flowers." If he'd been so coldhearted...so brazen as to contact Mr. Bonomo and place an order. If he'd used the same florist he'd bought her flowers from a hundred times over their years together. The fact that he hadn't changed nothing. In fact, she almost wished he had. Then it would've been easier. Then she could've hated his guts for humiliating her even more.

But for the first time, instead of being sad or angry at Paul, she felt terrified. If Paul was such a great guy—and by all accounts, he was—then maybe it wasn't his fault he'd turned to another woman.

Maybe it was hers.

She pushed the thought to the back of her mind to pull out and explore later. To press and prod, like a fresh bruise. Her son was due at the clinic any minute and she needed to get herself together.

"I thank you for being honest with me, Bryan. I know it can't have been easy. He was your best friend and this has to be upsetting. I'll do as you said, take some time and let this sink in. In the meantime, I'll call and make an appointment with that therapist."

"That sounds like a good idea," Bryan said with a nod. "I know this isn't what you wanted to hear, but I at least hope it gives you some closure. Sometimes, the not knowing is the worst part."

Judging by the gaping wound in her chest that used to be her heart, she was pretty sure he was wrong on that front, but she knew he was trying to be kind, so she forced a nod.

"I'm definitely grateful you told me. I still don't feel like I have closure yet, though. I have some questions I still need answered, and I'm hoping this woman can provide them. Once I take a step back and regroup, I'm going to push ahead and try to locate her."

"Are you sure that's wise, Steph?" Bryan asked, his face a mask of concern. "Maybe at least talk to the therapist first. It seems like knowing all the torrid details would hurt more than help."

"Maybe so, but I think what my imagination is providing might be even worse."

Christine Gael and Denise Grover Swank

"At least let me know when you locate her and consider letting me act as a buffer. You don't know this woman at all. You said she and Paul may have had a falling-out. What if she's crazy? Or vindictive? You've been through enough."

She couldn't argue there. She felt like she'd been through hell and back, with no end in sight. And what if she was wrong about Paul being alive? What if she tried to confront his lover and found him there with her after all?

Maybe Bryan was right. But now wasn't the time for making decisions.

"I'll definitely keep you posted." She paused and glanced down at her watch. "I've got to get back."

They made the short walk back to the clinic together, and Bryan climbed into his car after making her promise to keep in contact.

He was just pulling away as Todd pulled in. Stephanie manufactured a smile and waved to her son. He hopped out of the car with a wide smile, pointing down to his brand-new white lab coat with his name stitched across the pocket in blue.

Todd Ketterman, DVM.

"Well?"

Her throat felt like it was closing up, but she managed to reply. "Amazing. I'm so proud of you, Todd."

"I'm pretty psyched myself. It seemed like it was never going to happen." A cloud passed over his handsome, smiling face. "I only wish Dad were alive to see it."

And just like that, the hairline cracks in her carefully constructed wall came tumbling down in a heap of rubble as a sob bubbled from her throat.

"Mom?"

130

Todd ran toward her as she lowered herself on the cement step in front of the door, tears streaming down her face.

"I'm sorry. God, I'm so sorry. I just can't . . ."

"Is it Aunt Anna? Mom, what's going on?" Todd demanded, dropping to a squat before her and pulling her into his arms.

He held her tight as she wept, breathing in the comforting scent of his shampoo, trying to get a grip. It took a solid five minutes before she could speak, and even then, she didn't know what she was going to say until she said it. Like all mothers, she wanted to protect her children from any pain. But she and Todd would be working side by side, every day. There was no way she could hide this from him. Not entirely.

Not anymore.

"Todd…I have something I need to tell you. It's about your father."

As she began to tell her son what the last few months had unearthed, she was already thinking ahead to later that evening.

The second she got home, she was going to call the therapist Ethan recommended, Dr. Reva Yang. Because if ever she needed to talk to an objective person who had the ability to prescribe antidepressant medication, it was now…

Chapter Fifteen

Cee-cee stood in front of her living room window, overlooking the harbor. She loved this view. When she'd moved out of the contemporary home she and Nate had built several years ago, she knew she wouldn't miss the house itself. The house was pure Nate, but she knew she'd miss the ocean view. Watching the waves recharged her. Filled her soul, so she was thrilled that her apartment came with the bakery retail space below. She had to admit that she wasn't a fan of the stairs—especially when she had to take her little dog Tilly out to potty before bed. Her apartment was on the second floor from the street but third from the walkout basement. Thankfully, her boyfriend Mick stayed over often and volunteered to take Tilly out. And she'd gotten her view. She was winning on all fronts.

Cee-cee thought about her life now compared to her life a year ago, and she felt like she'd woken up from a bad dream. A year ago, she'd been meek and mild Celia Burrows, Nate's dutiful wife, Gabe and Max's mother. She'd lost herself along the way, so much so that when Nate said he was leaving her and moving in with his new girlfriend, she'd struggled to figure out what she wanted to do. When she'd found Nate's note, she thought it was the worst thing to ever happen to her. Instead, it turned out to be the best.

Now she had her own thriving cupcake shop, which had gained exposure when she'd participated in and won a television baking show. She had a loving, thoughtful partner who did everything in his power to make her happy. Days like today, she couldn't believe how lucky she was.

Steph had been lucky. She'd found the love of her life in college, had her dream job as a vet with her own practice. Three healthy, thoughtful children who now had successful careers of their own. Then, in the blink of an eye, she'd lost Paul and instead of mourning and finding a way to move forward, she was now stuck in a downward spiral of grief and doubt.

How had that happened?

"Hey," Mick said, coming up behind her. He pressed his chest to her back and wrapped his arms around her abdomen, tugging her close. "You seem like you're a million miles away," he whispered in her ear.

She turned her head and glanced back up him. "Just thinking about Steph."

He squeezed her tighter, and she turned in his arms, placing her hands on his chest. "Thank you."

A smile spread across his face. "For what?"

"For making dinner. For rubbing my feet. For taking Tilly out when it's dark." She placed a gentle kiss on his lips, then smiled up at him. "Thank you for being you."

He continued to smile down at her, but his smile wavered. "Then why do I see doubt in your eyes?"

Her gaze dropped to his chest. "It's nothing. It's stupid."

"Hey," he said, lifting her chin so her gaze met his. "If it's bothering you, it's not stupid."

"It's not *one* thing. It's a lot of things."

"I've got nothing but time to listen." He tugged her to the sofa and sat down, pulling her down next to him, wrapping an arm around her until she was plastered to his side. "What's going on in that beautiful head of yours?"

"Max told me that she thinks Nate is unhappy with Amanda."

She felt him momentarily stiffen, but then his tension eased.

"Do you still want me to share this?" she prodded.

"Cee-cee, if it's on your mind, and you want to share, I want to hear it."

"She said that Amanda and her dog's high energy are getting to him, and that she doesn't think he'll last there much longer. She says she thinks he realizes he made a mistake leaving me."

"And do you think he made a mistake?" Mick asked carefully.

Leaning closer into him, she gave him a grin. "I think he made the biggest mistake of his life. If you're asking if I want to go back to him—I'd rather shove bamboo sticks under my fingernails. It took him leaving for me to realize how much I'd shelved my own needs and wants. That my opinion matters."

A frown creased his brow. "I hope you never think I discount your needs and wants."

"Are you kidding?" she asked with a gasp. "You're the most attentive man I know." Then she frowned...*other than Paul*. She pressed on. "Actually, I don't think him leaving me was a mistake. I'm not sure what Nate needs in a mate, but I obviously wasn't it, and he wasn't mine. He did us both a favor, and if he gets free from Amanda, then maybe he'll be able to find out who that is."

He chuckled. "That's mighty mature of you."

"It's taken me a while to reach this point," she admitted. "But most of my bitterness is gone." She gave him another kiss. "How can I be bitter when him leaving brought me to you? It's the best gift he could have given me."

"I love you, Cee-cee," Mitch said in a husky voice.

"I love you too."

He gave her a long lazy kiss that spoke of their intimacy, not just physically, but emotionally. Cee-cee had grown to trust him, count on him, need him. That might have scared her soon after her breakup with Nate, but she knew that Mick felt the same about her. That he was happy only if she was happy, and vice versa.

"Do you think that it's possible for two people deeply in love to lose each other along the way?" she asked, draped over his chest.

"Sure," he said, lifting a hand to brush hair from her cheek. Then his hand lingered there. "But it takes work. Just like you and I are trying to do."

She nodded. "But do you think a couple can appear to be in love, and one of them cheat on the other?"

"This is about Paul, isn't it?" he asked gently.

"He and Steph just seemed so devoted to one another. Still in love after thirty years together. If they couldn't keep it together, then it makes me wonder about . . ."

"Us?" he asked.

She looked up into his neutral eyes and cringed. "I guess."

"There are no guarantees, Cee-cee. We can only both commit to communicating and making each other a priority. As we both know, relationships take a lot of work. I think we both are committed to this."

"We are," she mused, but she couldn't help realizing that while they'd said the L word months ago, they'd never discussed what their mutual future looked like. She presumed together. Mick talked like he presumed together, but there'd been no actual discussion. Maybe it was time.

"Where do you see us in five years?" she asked.

His eyes widened slightly, obviously caught off guard by her question. "You mean careers? Or us?"

"Us. We're talking about us and committing. We've never talked about it, so I wondered."

He shifted on the sofa to face her. "Are you talking about being together or a formal commitment like marriage?"

It was her turn to be uncomfortable, but then she grinned playfully. "I guess I'd kind of like to know what your intentions are, Mick Rafferty."

He laughed in his low-timbred voice, which sent ripples of happiness through her. She equated his laugh to love and acceptance and pure joy. She'd rarely laughed with Nate, and now she laughed multiple times a day with Mick.

"It's not a big deal," she said. "All this commitment talk got me thinking about it, is all. I'm happy with the way things are now."

"I'm happy too," he said, "but that doesn't mean I'm content with the way things are. I want more with you, Cee-cee. I want a formal commitment." He picked up her left hand. "And I'm willing to admit that there's a caveman part of me that wants to see you wearing a ring I gave you on your third finger."

She sucked in a breath. "An engagement ring?"

"To start," he said. "And for a very short time before I convince you to officially become my wife."

"You hadn't breathed a word of any of that," she said. "I had no idea."

He cupped her cheek. "You had to know that I'm crazy about you."

"I did, but . . ."

"When I'm not with you, Cee-cee, you're always there in the back of my mind, and I'm counting the hours until I can be with you again."

"But you never once hinted that you wanted to get married."

"To be fair," he said, "neither have you. I figured that was on purpose. You just got out of an unfulfilling thirty-year marriage. I didn't want you to feel trapped in a marriage with me."

"I would never feel trapped with you, Mick," she said, placing her hand over his, which still rested on her cheek. "I consider every moment with you to be a gift. I guess I've never mentioned marriage because you've never been married. I know you've had girlfriends before, and I know you said the relationships ended before you got to that stage, but part of me couldn't help wondering if you were averse to it."

Shaking his head, a soft smile lit up his eyes. "I'm not averse to marriage, Cee-cee. I was just waiting for the right woman. I guess I've been waiting for you."

Tears blurred her eyes and her heart swelled.

"But you haven't even been divorced a year. I wanted to give you time. The last thing I want is for you to feel rushed."

"I'm not feeling rushed," she said. "Everything seems to be occurring at the right pace." She made a face. "I feel a little foolish now, thinking you might not want to marry me." He started to say something, but she held up her hand.

"And I was okay with that. As long as we're together, that's what really matters. Not a marriage license and a ring."

He smiled. "But I want the marriage license and the ring."

"And so do I."

He kissed her again, and she couldn't help thinking about all the wasted years with Nate. He'd never once made her feel like this. Not even in the beginning. But all those years had led her to Mick. If she'd broken up with Nate earlier, Mick might have been in one of his previous relationships and she might have met someone else. Cee-cee was practical enough to think that there wasn't one perfect person in the world for everyone, but she was smart enough to realize that Mick was as close to perfect for her as she could imagine.

"About Paul…," he said with a grimace. "I knew him fairly well. And I saw him with Stephanie. I'm telling you, Cee-cee, there's no way he was having an affair. He worshiped his wife, and I have to confess the way you and your sisters are jumping on this bandwagon is not only surprising but disappointing. I only hope if something similar happens to me, you'll trust me and our relationship and not jump to conclusions." He made a face and looked chastised even though she hadn't said a word. "And that's the last time I'll bring it up. You asked, so I just had to share my honest thoughts. Now I'll retreat to my own corner and let you girls work it out."

"It's not that easy, Mick," she said, feeling chastised herself, but there was no anger with him. She couldn't help thinking that maybe he had a point. "But I've decided—even before your lecture—that you're right. I felt obligated to tell Steph what Prue said about Paul. But the more I think about it, the more I remember about the two of them together, the more I don't think Paul was having an affair either." She drew back and took a steadying breath. "But I do know we need to get to the bottom of it or Steph will never be able to find peace."

Chapter Sixteen

Steph had been a mess since telling Todd about his father. She still wondered if it had been a selfish move, that she stole the persona of the man Todd had thought his father to be, but he'd insisted that he wanted to know. And, frankly, she hadn't been able to hold it together well enough to deny him. She'd apologized profusely in the aftermath.

"In case you haven't noticed," he'd said, trying to strike a jovial tone and failing miserably. "I'm not a child anymore, Mom. I'm a grown man who's about to join your practice. You don't need to hide things from me, and you don't need to protect me."

"I'll always want to protect you," she'd said.

"And I appreciate it, but maybe you should let me help instead of shutting me out. I know I've been gone for eight years getting my college degree and in vet school, but I'm home now. I'm ready to step up, both at the clinic and with my family."

His words had soothed her to some degree, but she still hadn't shaken all of the guilt. Thankfully, the therapist had fit her in on Friday afternoon, and Steph had spent most of the fifty minutes pouring out her heartache and pain while the therapist, a tiny young woman who didn't look a day over twenty-five, listened patiently and took notes, stopping Steph occasionally to ask questions. Finally, Steph finished regurgitating her feelings and said, "I need help. I think I'm losing my mind."

Dr. Yang gave her a warm smile and said reassuringly, "You can put that worry aside. You're not crazy. You're dealing with a trauma and everyone deals with it differently. You're still in shock over all of this, and while I can't tell you if your husband cheated or not, I do know that how you handle this is entirely up to you. It's not to make light of your feelings, but merely to tell you that you can learn to overcome this. You don't have to be a victim, Stephanie. You can take ownership of your own healing."

Steph had nodded dumbly, loving the sound of that, but she felt so deep at the bottom of the pool of despair, she had no idea how she was going to find the surface. When she told the therapist that thought, the woman chuckled softly.

"We'll work on it together. I could put you on a low dose of antidepressants, but I prefer not to use them in cases of situational depression, like you're experiencing now. I find that therapy itself is usually the best way to handle it. In the meantime, try to be kind to yourself. Indulge yourself. Maybe that's a mani-pedi, or a massage, or maybe it's giving yourself permission to eat a pint of gourmet ice cream. Say yes to good things. Let yourself have fun. Your homework before our next session is for you to pamper yourself. I'll expect a full report when we meet."

"Okay," Steph had said, and the timer went off. She'd made an appointment to meet with Dr. Yang on Wednesday, and left, feeling slightly better.

On Saturday, she shadowed Todd on the cases that came in. She knew he'd been trained well, but they'd both agreed to the arrangement until he felt comfortable. But Todd knew what he was doing and had an excellent tableside manner with the clients, leaving her plenty of time to let her mind wander.

She hadn't come up with her splurge yet, and being the type A person she was, she was overthinking it. While she knew Dr. Yang didn't care what she did—the purpose of the exercise was simply to find enjoyment in something, anything—Steph didn't want it to be lame. She wanted it to have substance.

And finding enough substance to take her mind off the bombshell Bryan had dropped earlier that week was going to be a task.

She was surprised at how well Todd was taking it. While the news of Paul's possible infidelity had caught him off guard and was clearly upsetting, he'd been nothing but supportive of her in the aftermath of their talk. He'd kept his own feelings guarded, only saying that he knew his father loved her with every part of his being. But he had been open to the possibility that maybe Paul had been going through a midlife crisis or had some weak moments, and supported Steph while she tried to decide on her next move. He'd also agreed to keep a lid on their discussion in regard to his siblings. At least until she knew more. Todd had been stoic, and Jeff might have been able to get on board with that, but Sarah would be a whole other story.

Daddy's little girl. She was already emotional about not having him around to walk her down the aisle in a few months. Sarah couldn't know until or unless there was some definitive proof.

"Want to get lunch after we wrap things up?" Todd asked her right before they went in to see their last patient—a beagle with an open wound on his leg that he wouldn't stop licking.

Steph's first reaction was to tell him no. She had a ton of errands to run that she'd put off all week. But Dr. Yang was in her ear. *Say yes to things that make you happy.* So she did.

Todd said he was feeling nostalgic, so they went to the diner and ordered lobster bisque and sourdough gouda grilled cheese sandwiches. Just like when he was a kid, but the memory sobered them both, bringing thoughts of Paul back to the forefront. In order to steer the conversation to something less maudlin, Steph changed the topic to her clinic. Todd told her that a lot of practices were now using electronic tablets when the vets saw patients and recorded the examination results in a veterinary program.

"I can look into how much it costs," he said. "See if you can afford it."

"*We* can afford it," she said with a smile. "We're bare-bones, but I think we can swing it. Especially since we'll be expanding the practice. Twice the veterinarians, twice the patients."

They finished their lunch and Steph decided to splurge on pie. Just as she was about to take a bite, she heard a familiar voice.

"Stephanie, I was just about to call you."

She glanced up to see Ethan Jenkins standing next to their table. Part of her was happy to see him. Despite the usual topic of their conversations, she'd come to think of him as a friend. But with Todd present and the recent information that she'd learned from Bryan, she felt a little uneasy at his sudden presence.

"Hello, Ethan. You here for some lunch?" she asked.

He thumbed toward the pickup counter. "I called in an order for lunch."

Steph caught Todd watching her with curiosity and her cheeks burned. "Ethan, this is my son, Doctor of Veterinary Medicine Todd Ketterman. He's returned home to join my practice. Todd, this is Detective Ethan Jenkins, with the Bluebird Bay Police. He's been helping me with the matter regarding your father."

Todd slid out of the booth and stood to greet him, extending his hand. "It's nice to meet you, Detective."

"Likewise," Ethan said, taking his hand and shaking.

"Thank you for helping my mother."

Ethan patted Todd's bicep. "More than happy to do it. In fact, that was why I planned to call you." He gestured to the table. "May I join you for a quick second...or if you'd rather step outside for a moment?"

"Todd is aware of everything. Please, sit," Steph said, scooting over on the booth seat to make room for him.

Ethan and Todd sat down and Todd leaned forward, eager to hear what the detective had to say.

"I got a call from my contact at the DMV, and I think we have a lead on a car that might have belonged to the mystery woman."

Steph's stomach dropped to her feet. "Oh my God! Who is she? Where is it?"

"About two hours north of here."

"Well, I want to come with you."

Ethan grimaced. "I don't know if that's a good idea."

"I need to come. I'll be able to recognize it."

Ethan shook his head dubiously. "It might be nothing. A total waste of time. I can just take a photo of it and send it."

"No," Steph said, adamant now. "I'm coming with you."

Steph and Ethan had a momentary staring contest until Todd interrupted: "One thing you should know about my mother, Detective, is that she's stubborn as the day is long. You might as well save time and just accept the fact that she's going with you."

Ethan grinned at her, an ornery grin that suggested he'd expected her to insist on coming all along. "Before you start volunteering, there *is* something else you should know. I need to meet with the car's current owner at eight-thirty a.m. in Linton, so I planned to cross over the Canadian border tonight and spend the night at the new casino there rather than getting up at the crack of dawn and driving. I won a free stay at the hotel there, and a hundred dollars' worth of chips. Still want to go?"

"Of course," Steph said, her head spinning. "Pop's night nurse will be there by five, and Todd is on call tomorrow. I think I can make it work." This would be one more step toward the closure she needed. Plus, Dr. Yang's voice was still in her head, so she added, "Maybe I'll even gamble at the casino while we're there."

Ethan looked pleased. "I'll share half of my chips with you."

"Who are you and what have you done with my mother?" Todd asked with a shake of his head and a bemused smile.

Steph lifted her chin. "I can gamble."

She never had, but it wasn't too late to start.

Ethan didn't look deterred. "It's a two-hour drive," he said, "so how about I pick you up from your house at four?"

"Sounds good," she said. "I'll see you then."

TWO HOURS LATER, Steph's stomach was churning as she carried her overnight bag to the living room. She told herself it was because she was anxious to find out if the car had belonged to the mystery woman, and if it had, what might be salvageable from it, but that was only part of her angst. The other part was this strange feeling she got in her belly whenever Ethan was around.

Ethan.

When had he stopped being Detective Jenkins in her mind?

"How well do you really know this guy?" Todd asked, frown lines wrinkling his forehead. "Should you really be going on an overnight trip with him?" Then he added emphatically, "Out of the country?"

"For heaven's sake," Steph said. "It's Canada. It barely qualifies as another country."

"You need your passport to cross the border, so yes. You are leaving the country."

"I'm a grown woman, Todd. I know how to take care of myself."

"But this is going to be stressful twofold. You've got the mysterious car to worry about, and plus, you haven't dated in over thirty years, so I'd say you're rusty. I just want to make sure you're mentally prepared."

"Date?" she stammered in shock. "This is not a date."

"I saw the way that man was looking at you, Mom. It may not be an official date, but he wants it to be."

She snorted. "Don't be ridiculous." She glanced out the front door and saw a sedan pull into the driveway. "There's Ethan. I've got to go. Thanks for watching Pop until the night nurse shows up. I'll text later to let you know that I haven't been serial-murdered." Then she kissed his cheek and rushed out the door, all the while wondering herself . . .

Was this a date?

And if it was, would that be so bad?

Chapter Seventeen

Max was nervous. She hadn't been on a date since the disastrous ending to her relationship with Robbie. She had known it wasn't a long-term commitment. Robbie was an artist with a studio and gallery a block down the main Bluebird Bay strip. She'd met him at a First Friday and the next thing she knew, they were in a relationship. It had started out as pure physical attraction—a couple-of-times fling—but then it lasted longer, and before she knew it, she was in a semi-relationship with him that helped fill her loneliness. But what had started out as fun had ended up controlling and selfish and had culminated in Robbie striking her in a restaurant parking lot in front of several witnesses.

She hadn't dated since. Partially because she'd put her all into saving her struggling business, partially because she and her mother had been spending more time together, and partially because she was scared to start another relationship. Never in a million years would she have expected Robbie to turn into a controlling, abusive boyfriend. What if she picked another guy who ended up like Robbie?

Then she'd seen Tyler at the bar and all those fears had faded away. Memories of their high school years had flooded her head, and nostalgia had taken over, encouraging her to accept his invitation to dinner.

But now, as she waited for him to show up at her apartment, she was having serious misgivings. She still didn't have time to start a relationship. She needed to put all her time and energy into the bookstore or she would lose everything.

Just as she was seriously considering texting Tyler to tell him that she'd come down with the flu, she heard a rap at the front door.

When she opened the door, Tyler stood in front of her, his eyes widening at the sight of her.

"Max, you look beautiful."

She blushed. "Thank you." And just as she was about to tell him she couldn't go with him, she took a long look at him. Tyler was a handsome man. With his dark, wavy hair and crystal blue eyes, he could likely have his pick of any woman he wanted…if he actually left the bar and hung out with people his age. But it was the kindness in his eyes and the feeling of comfort that she sensed from him that stopped her. Something about him said she could trust him.

"You ready to go to dinner? I thought we could go to Pietro's."

The name caught her off guard. The place her uncle Paul had met up with his supposed mistress on the morning of his death.

"They have an impressive wine list," he said when she didn't react.

Going to Pietro's could be good. The scene of the crime, so to speak. "No, it sounds lovely. I've never been there."

"Neither have I, so it's going to be a first for both of us. Something that's hard to accomplish since we both grew up here," he said with a boyish grin.

They headed out and he said, "I ordered an Uber to drive us. I want to be responsible, but I also want to be able to enjoy the wine list."

"Of course," she said eagerly, pleased that he'd thought of it, because she sure hadn't.

The SUV was waiting at the curb, and Tyler opened the car door and waited to get in beside her. They chatted during the half-hour drive to the restaurant, sharing what they knew about their mutual friends and what they were up to. Tyler's hand rested on the seat next to his leg, and Max spent most of the drive thinking his hand was so close to hers yet so far.

After the Uber pulled into the crowded parking lot, Tyler got out and held the door open for her. Once they were inside the restaurant, Tyler placed a hand at the small of her back when they entered the crowded foyer.

Tingles shot up her back, and she turned to see if he'd felt it too, only to meet his own surprised eyes.

She smiled at him and he smiled back, wrapping his arm around her back, his hand resting on her hip as he guided her through the throng toward the hostess stand.

"I have reservations at 7:30," he told the young woman behind the stand. "Tyler Martin."

She checked her tablet and glanced up at him with a smile as she grabbed two menus. "Welcome to Pietro's, Mr. Martin. Follow me and I'll get you seated."

She led the way and Max and Tyler followed her, Tyler's hand still on Max's hip even though there weren't any obstacles in their path.

She couldn't deny, it felt nice.

He held out her chair when they reached their table, then sat across from her, staring at her with wonderment and adoration.

Butterflies took flight in Max's stomach and a soft smile spread across her face.

"Are you celebrating a special occasion?" the hostess asked.

"Nope," Tyler said, keeping his gaze on Max's face. "First date."

"You two look this in love on your first date?" she asked in awe. "I sure hope you have your first anniversary here. I can't wait to see you then." She released a chuckle. "Your server will be right with you, not that you'd notice if he took too long," she teased as she walked away.

"That's the second time someone has said something like that to me about you," Max said. "Lydia was the first." Then realizing what she'd said, she hastily added, "I hope that doesn't freak you out and send you running."

He shook his head, still smiling. "Nope. I'm not going anywhere."

The waiter brought the menus and stood quietly waiting as they took a moment to peruse the wine list. Tyler ordered a glass of Riesling to start, then gave Max an expectant look.

She flashed him a warm smile. "Please. I'm dining with a sommelier. I'm letting you order for me." She glanced up at the waiter. "I'll have the Riesling too."

They looked over the menu and Tyler compared it to the wine list.

When the waiter returned with their wine and a basket of warm bread, they placed their orders for prime rib and surf and turf, and Tyler ordered a bottle of cabernet sauvignon to go with their meals.

Tyler lifted his wine glass as the waiter walked off with their order, and held it toward Max. She lifted her glass to his.

"May this be the start of something wonderful."

She clicked her glass with his, and the butterflies were back. She was relieved she wasn't the only one of them feeling this way.

A short while later, the waiter brought out their food and the bottle of wine they'd selected. When he left, Tyler told Max why he chose that particular wine and label and how it paired with their meal. Max smiled at his enthusiasm as he talked about full body and oaky notes.

"Sorry," he said with a grimace. "I tend to get too excited. Most people don't get it and find it annoying and pretentious. I hope I haven't screwed this up already."

Max laughed. "No. I love it. You're obviously very passionate about food and wine, and you're obviously very well educated if you became a sommelier. It must have been hard to give that all up to take over running your father's bar." She squinted at him, narrowing her eyes. "How'd you get off on a Saturday night, anyway?"

"I had one of the weeknight bartenders switch with me. And thank you for your understanding. In the future, I'll try to rein it in."

Leaning forward, she said, "Don't you dare. The only way we'll ever work is if we don't hide ourselves, and besides," she added with a smile, "I like watching you get excited, and I know nothing about wine, so I find it fascinating. Please don't stop."

"You just might regret telling me that," he teased.

"I doubt it, but how about this? If I ever find it annoying, I'll find a gentle way to let you know."

"Deal."

She asked him about how he became interested in food and wine, and he told her it started in his father's bar and watching the Food Network in high school.

"I had no idea," she said. "I don't think anyone did."

"That's because I didn't tell anyone. While everyone was planning which college to go to, I was searching for culinary schools. My father wasn't happy with my decision. He told me I'd never use my fancy cooking at Petey's." He leaned his head to the side. "And sure enough, he was right."

"I hate that you're not doing what you love," she said.

"Are you doing what you love?" he asked. "Has it been your lifelong dream to own a bookstore?"

"Not exactly," she said, "but I realized the corporate accounting world wasn't for me, and I was dying to have a reason to come back home. So I quit my job and opened a bookstore, and while I was in the process of working on the building, my mother decided to open a cupcake shop several blocks down the street. She'd been a stay-at-home mom for years, my father cheated on her and left, and she had a mini identity crisis and decided to open a cupcake shop." She grimaced. "Now I know this sounds terrible, but while I hoped she did well, I truly thought I'd do better than her. I was the one who had taken business classes in school. I'm a CPA; she entertained my father's business clients. So when her business took off and mine floundered, I was not only shocked, but humiliated."

"Humiliated?" he asked, surprised. "Why?"

She leaned closer and playfully lifted her brow. "I'm not sure if you remember this about me, but I'm an overachiever. And I'm highly competitive. And my middle-aged mother with absolutely no business sense doing better than me?" She shrugged. "I was upset. And jealous. And a whole host of other terrible things."

Tilting her head to the side, she asked, "Still like me now?" Then she finished off her glass of wine, sure she'd blown it.

"You think admitting that you're human's going to run me off?" he asked, pouring more wine into her glass. "I did know you were competitive in high school, and you don't become a CPA by being a slacker. So I wouldn't expect anything less."

"You're not surprised I'm jealous of my mother's successful business?"

"No, I'm not surprised that what you see as failing deeply hurts you."

"But what kind of daughter does that make me?"

"A human one, Max. If I were starting a business at the same time as my father, it would bother me if his business was thriving and mine was struggling."

She glanced down at her plate, asking herself what on earth had possessed her to admit this to him.

"Max."

She looked back up at him.

"You're a beautiful person inside and out. You're entitled to your feelings, even the bad ones."

A slow smile spread across her face. "Now you sound like a therapist."

"Maybe I've heard it myself," he said. "I had a lot of feelings after my brother's death. Some I'm not so proud of. It's part of life."

"Tyler, I'm so sorry. My business issues pale in comparison to what happened to your brother."

"You're putting your whole heart into your business," Tyler said. "It's an important part of you. And I have some ideas that might benefit us both, but no business tonight. We can talk about that later."

As eager as she was to hear the details of his plan, she liked that he wanted to keep business separate. She didn't want to think about the depressing bottom line of the bookstore right now. She just wanted to be here, in this moment, and enjoy some time with this amazing guy.

They continued talking throughout the meal. Max ordered a fat slab of death by chocolate cake for them to share as well as a coffee to go with the dessert wine.

"I can't believe I've never been here before," she said, sipping on her coffee. "And no one I'm close to has been for me to hear how good it is."

"Your mom or your aunts haven't been?" he asked in surprise.

"Not that I know of." She frowned. "But apparently my uncle Paul was here the morning of his death."

Tyler's mouth dropped open. "What?"

"Yeah," she said with a sigh. "It's a long story, but the short version was that some busybody saw him here with a woman, told my mother, who told Aunt Stephanie. As you can imagine, it caused quite the stir."

"Wasn't your uncle Paul Ketterman?"

"One and the same."

"He was with a woman here?"

"A breakfast meeting," Max said.

"Do you know what she looks like?" He shook his head. "This is going to sound weird, but I came back home to help fill in for my dad when he had an outpatient surgery." He scrunched his nose, clearly deep in thought. "I guess it was about three years ago? I was working a double. I'd finished the lunch shift and wanted to grab a container of chowder and sit out on the pier to eat...take a breather before I went back for the night shift. It was around three o'clock and the place was dead. I was just about to head out of the bar when I saw Paul and a blonde woman who wasn't Stephanie sitting in a corner booth. I thought it was odd that they came in midafternoon."

Max set down her forkful of cake and swallowed hard. "Oh my gosh. That means he met with a blonde woman twice at a restaurant. And also in a park. Aunt Stephanie has convinced herself that he was having an affair. Did you see them doing anything that hinted it was a romantic relationship?

He shook his head. "No. They sat in a back corner table, but they weren't touching. In fact, they seemed to keep their distance. He handed her some papers and she looked them over, then folded them up and put them in her purse. They talked a bit longer, then left soon after."

"So it looked like a business meeting?" she asked.

"No, more like he was her handler." When she gave him a blank look, he said, "You know when a handler is meeting with his or her informant."

She froze for a moment, then dove into her purse to find her phone. "I'm sorry," she said as she pulled up her aunt's number. "But I have to tell my aunt about this right away."

"Of course," he said.

The phone rang several times, and when it went to voicemail, Max could hear her aunt's voice in her ear. "This is Stephanie Ketterman, and I'm out of town for the weekend. If this is a veterinary emergency, call Todd Ketterman at 555–2853. If this is a personal call, leave a message and I'll get back to you when I come back to the U.S."

Max lowered her phone and stared at the screen to verify it was her aunt's number, even though she'd confirmed it with the message. Then she realized the phone had beeped, alerting her to leave her message.

"Hey, Aunt Steph, I can't believe you left the country...that's just so unlike you." She shook her head. "Anyway, call me when you get a chance. I've got something important to tell you."

When she hung up, she glanced out the window, trying to make sense of her aunt's sudden trip. Did her mother know? She was half tempted to call her, but instead she slipped her phone into her purse. If Aunt Stephanie had gone away, she clearly needed a break from all this. No point in getting everyone in an uproar. Besides, she was having the perfect night with a darn near perfect man. It could wait until the morning.

Chapter Eighteen

"This place is unreal," Stephanie marveled as they stepped into the elevator of the glamorous hotel lobby. When she and Ethan had pulled up to the sleek set of attached buildings and not one but two valets had run up to open their doors and help them with their overnight bags, she'd known the place was going to be swanky. But as she'd walked around the lobby looking at the myriad crystal chandeliers and posh decor while Ethan had checked them in, she'd realized that this might be the nicest place she'd ever stayed in. She and Paul had traveled a dozen or more times over their years together, so that was saying something.

The elevator slid smoothly from floor to floor, finally stopping at 21.

"This is us," Ethan said, holding the door open and gesturing for her to go first. They followed a sign to their room number and slowed as they reached the door. She'd been so nervous when he'd first picked her up, she'd forgotten to ask about sleeping arrangements. And once they'd cranked the radio and played name that tune most of the two-hour ride up here, it had been so fun and easy, she hadn't thought about it again.

Until now.

Her palms went clammy as Ethan used a card key to open the door. She was almost afraid to look inside. What if there was only one bed? How would she broach that without seeming awkward? What she found there, though, set her mind instantly at ease.

Two luxuriously appointed queen beds in the center of a massive room overlooking the water.

"Wow," she murmured as she hurried toward the window. "That view is breathtaking. You got this room for free?" Even the fully stocked minibar was packed with fancy items. No peanuts and M&M's here. This was serious business, complete with macadamia nuts and chocolates shaped like a splayed deck of cards courtesy of a local chocolatier.

"Actually, once I convinced you to come, I called and upgraded," Ethan admitted with a sheepish chuckle. "I know this isn't technically a date, but I can't deny it. I wanted to impress you."

She turned to face him, grinning from ear to ear, rocked to her core and thrilled to her toes by his honesty. Despite the unfortunate circumstances of their initial meeting, getting to know this man had been a pleasure so far. And something told her she'd only scratched the surface.

If only she could truly let go of the past and focus on the future, maybe there could be something more than friendship between them…

She pushed away the sudden image of Paul's face, along with all the crushing guilt, grief, and doubt that came with it, and set her purse down on the nightstand.

"Well, it worked. I'm impressed. Now, what do you say we crack open some of these little bottles—that will be my treat—mix some drinks, and then we head down and try our luck?"

Ethan grinned back at her and made his way toward the mini bar. "Sounds like a plan." He whipped up a pair of Scotch and sodas while they talked. It took a few minutes for Stephanie to bring it up because the last thing she wanted to do was ruin their evening before it even started, but eventually, she had to ask.

"I'm trying not to think about it, and I don't want it to be the focal point of our evening, but what do you think the chances are that this is the same car that Paul's assistant saw leaving the park that day?"

He let out a sigh and shrugged. "Maybe fifty-fifty. I realize in hindsight maybe I should've gone without telling you and confirmed before I mentioned it, but when I saw you out, I——" He broke off and raked a hand through his hair with a groan. "I'm ashamed to admit, I wondered who the guy you were with was. By the time I realized it was your son, I'd already sort of let the cat out of the bag. And I have to say, as much as I hate to disappoint you if things don't pan out tomorrow morning, I'm glad you're here now."

Her throat went dry and she clasped her hands together to keep them from trembling. This was all so new...so strange. She hadn't felt this way about a man except Paul since high school, and it was wreaking havoc on her insides.

"Well, for what it's worth, I'm not angry or upset with you. I want to be part of the whole process. I've had more than enough of secrets in my life. I want the truth at all times, no matter how painful that might be."

He gave her a grim nod. "I understand completely. And I promise I'll honor that request going forward."

"On that note, I have something I didn't mention. I'm not even sure why I've kept it to myself...maybe because I'm worried it reflects poorly on me somehow, and your opinion matters." She cleared her throat and pinned her attention to a spot over his shoulder, unable to meet his gaze. "Paul's business partner looked into his expense accounts leading up to the date of his death. There were some disturbing charges. For flowers…and hotel rooms that didn't make sense."

Ethan let out a muffled curse and shook his head slowly. "Geez, Stephanie, I'm so sorry. I know that couldn't have been easy to hear. But please know that doesn't change my opinion of you in the least. Your husband's choices were his own. I've seen nothing but a beautiful, bright, engaging woman who deserves nothing less than a man's everything. I'm sorry you have doubts that your husband felt that way in light of all this."

"Thank you, Ethan," she murmured, her lips tipping into a trembling smile. "I feel like a weight has been lifted off me now that I've said it all out loud," she admitted, finally meeting his eyes again. "So what do you say we put this whole nightmare into a box for the rest of the evening now and just enjoy this amazing place?"

"Sounds like a plan to me."

With the elephant in the room out of the way, Ethan deftly maneuvered their discussion to lighter topics. Her career and love of animals, his job and penchant for public service and his time in the military. They wound up lounging on the beds opposite one another, talking and eating macadamia nuts for over an hour before they put it into gear and set their glasses down.

"Ever try your hand at craps?" he asked, raising one brow in a challenge.

"I have not, but I'm a quick learner, if you're willing to show me the ropes."

He stood and reached out a hand to help her to her feet. The second his big, strong hand closed over hers, she knew it for sure.

They could both declare it "not a date" all they wanted. This was a date.

And damned if she wasn't positively giddy to see where it might lead.

For the next few hours, it was a whirlwind of activity. They hit the craps table first, with mixed results. Once he'd explained the basics to her, Ethan slid over half of his casino-comped chips and they began to play. Ethan had lost fifty dollars within the first ten minutes, but Stephanie had taken a less orthodox approach, wagering small amounts on long-shot bets like snake eyes and hard fours. If she was going to gamble for the first time, she was going to go all out.

When she crowed with excitement as the croupier pushed yet another pile of chips her way, Ethan clapped obligingly, delighted for her.

"And just like that, the student becomes the master," he chuckled, shaking his head in awe.

"More like beginner's luck, but I'll take it." She scooped up her chips and split the pile into two, holding one out for him.

"Your half of my take. You staked me, after all."

He looked like he was going to argue, and she glared at him. "Remember what my son told you about me being stubborn?"

Ethan inclined his head and accepted the chips, and promptly rose another rung in her estimation. She'd spent far too long in the company of chauvinistic men. First, growing up with her father, whose lifelong dream it was to have three sons and who, upon having three daughters instead, wished that each of his girls would spend their days barefoot and pregnant. Then, at her first job as a part-time receptionist during the summers where she was told that her pantsuits were too masculine and she was instructed to wear pantyhose and skirts every day. And last, in college where a good number of her male counterparts talked over her and spent their time mansplaining concepts to her that she already knew back to front. It was one of the many things she'd loved about Paul. From the second they'd met, he'd treated her like his equal. He was a gentleman while still respecting her independence. A rare breed for men of her generation.

Now here was Ethan, courteous as could be, opening doors for her and treating her to this lovely trip, but also confident enough within himself to accept the gifts she offered him as well.

She liked that.

A lot.

"Where next? Want to try your hand at blackjack or roulette?"

She'd been lucky guessing numbers at craps, so they applied that silly logic to their decision-making process and ended up at the roulette wheel. Ethan stuck to his conservative approach, betting on red or black with each spin of the wheel. Stephanie continued to tempt fate, selecting a number on a whim before each spin. She lost all but thirty dollars of her money and was about to wave the white flag of surrender when she turned toward Ethan.

"What's your birth date?" she asked with a grin.

"March 14th. Yours?"

She gaped at him and reeled back with a bark of laughter. "You're joking. Tell me you're just being funny?!"

He shot her a bemused smile. "Nope, that's it. March 14th. Why?"

"March 14th."

His eyes went almost as wide as his grin. "Well, it seems like we have a lucky number in mind, don't we?"

She dropped three red five-dollar chips on the number fourteen and the others on the number three. Chuckling, Ethan did the same.

"Ooh, taking risks this time. I like it!" she teased.

"No more bets," the attractive woman behind the roulette table called as the wheel spun and the ball tripped wildly over the numbers.

Ethan leaned into her as they watched, his muscular arm and chest pressed against her side in a way that had her wondering if she was breathless, awaiting the ball to drop or from his nearness.

"Come on, baby. Daddy needs a new pair of shoes," Ethan called as the wheel slowed and the ball pitched from number to number. When it finally stopped, she let out a shriek.

"Holy crap! Fourteen! Fourteen!"

She wheeled around and launched herself into his waiting arms. He scooped her up like she weighed nothing at all and swung her in a giddy circle.

When he set her down, she couldn't help but marvel over how good he felt. How right.

"Congratulations. Fine job, you two!" the croupier cheered. She began scooping chips from the losing numbers before returning back to the cache of chips. "Do you want black?"

Stephanie and Ethan exchanged shocked smiles and nodded. Black chips were worth a hundred dollars apiece, and they'd each scored five of them and then some.

"This was the best idea ever," she said, clutching her winnings in her hand as they made their way from the table.

"It's turning out remarkably well," Ethan agreed as he slipped his chips into his pocket. "You getting hungry for dinner yet?"

"Sure," she said with a nod. "Lead the way."

He casually laced his fingers with hers and tugged her toward the casino exit that led into a long corridor full of shops and restaurants. Stephanie tried to focus on the food offerings as they tried to pick a cuisine, but all she could think about what how warm and strong Ethan's hand felt in hers.

The rest of the evening flew by in a whirlwind of laughter, fun, and yes...anticipation.

So when she and Ethan finally made their way back up to the hotel room, the silence that stretched between them as they stood eyeing both beds fairly pulsed with energy.

"Which bed would you prefer?" Ethan rasped, his low voice sending a tremor through her.

Tomorrow morning, she might find out for sure that everything she believed about her life was a lie. That the man she'd thought was her everything was nothing but a liar and a cheat. That her trust and love had been abused for decades. Maybe even that her dead husband might not be dead at all . . .

And if that happened? She'd be no good for anyone for a very long time as she tried to pick up the pieces. But she had here and now. They'd been gambling all night. Maybe they should see if their luck would hold up a little longer.

"We could share, if you like . . ."

Chapter Nineteen

I t should've been awkward. She'd kissed a man who wasn't Paul. She'd touched a man who wasn't Paul.

She'd slept in the arms of a man who wasn't Paul.

Instead, as they had moved around the hotel room the following morning packing their overnight bags in easy silence, all she felt was a bone-deep satisfaction. No doubt a large part of that was due to Ethan. He'd been so patient and sweet. When she'd almost second-guessed the whole thing as they'd undressed, he hadn't pressured her. And in the morning, he'd answered any question of whether this was a one-night fling or something more when she'd awoken to the smell of fresh coffee, warm croissants, and the feel of his lips pressed against hers.

"Good morning, sunshine," he'd murmured.

Even now, the memory of it warmed her from the inside out, which was a good thing because it helped thaw the icy block of fear lodged in her chest.

"You sure you want to do this?" Ethan asked softly as they made the last turn down a long dirt road toward Horace Breckenridge's house.

She wet her lips and nodded, the last of the warmth fading away. It had been a perfect night. One full of laughter and passion and joy. One she would never, ever forget. Maybe once they'd gotten past this meeting…once she'd finally gotten some closure, this thing between her and Ethan could move to the forefront. For now, though, it was on the back burner. In just a few minutes, she might very well find out the name of the woman her husband had been sharing hotel rooms with and sending flowers to.

"Yup. Very sure," she added as she sucked in a breath.

A small cabin came into view in the distance and she tensed.

"I know we've been over this, but I'm going to say it one more time for good measure. Until we have all the facts, try to remember the things you know are true deep in your soul, all right? Remember the beautiful children the two of you made. The way he looked at you on your wedding day. The laughter and joy you experienced together. No matter what he did the last few months of his life, a man doesn't fake that for decades, Stephanie. He loved you."

Emotion clogged her throat for two reasons. Partly because he was right. She knew it. Had felt it every day from her husband. But also because of Ethan. What kind of man spent the night with a woman he clearly had feelings for and then had the integrity and confidence to comfort her and reassure her about the feelings of her beloved deceased husband?

A good man. A man who deserved a woman who could be wholly present for him and him alone.

Tears flooded her eyes and she blinked them back furiously as they pulled into the gravel driveway.

"Ready?" Ethan asked softly, reaching out and squeezing her hand.

"Yup," she replied without hesitation.

They exited the car and headed up the pathway toward the front door, which swung open before they even reached the porch.

"Hi there. You must be Detective Jenkins," an elderly man croaked from behind a screen door. He smiled widely, flashing all three of his teeth. "And who's this pretty lady?"

"This is my friend, Stephanie Ketterman. She just came along for the ride," Ethan said casually. "May we come in?"

"Sure," Horace said, opening the door and stepping back to wave them in. "I can offer you water from the tap or the worst coffee you ever tasted. What'll it be?"

"I heard that, you old coot!" a cackling voice called from down the hall. "Keep talking and you can make your own dang coffee!"

Horace rolled his washed-out blue eyes and cupped his mouth to stage-whisper, "She says that every time, but she won't do it."

Oddly, Stephanie found the interplay between them comforting. It reminded her of Pop and Eva.

"Let's go right into the kitchen," Horace continued. "I promised her she wouldn't have to make an appearance on account of her still wearing her curlers and all."

"That'd be fine," Ethan said amiably as they followed the old man into a tiny, dated kitchen covered in wallpaper dotted with roosters.

"Coffee or water?" Horace asked again, one wiry gray brow arched.

"Nothing for me, thank you," Stephanie murmured. Her stomach was in knots and she didn't think she could swallow a thing.

"I'll take a cup of coffee," Ethan said.

"Brave man," Horace said with a wink as he hobbled around the kitchen prepping Ethan a chipped mug full of the blackest coffee Stephanie had ever seen.

Ethan accepted it with a nod of thanks and took a sip. "Tastes just like the stuff at the station. Tell the Mrs. I'm a fan."

"See, Horace? You've just got a bad palate is all," Horace's wife called back from down the hall.

Horace beamed and shook his head. "A charmer, huh? Well, good for you. Sit."

The three of them sat and Horace leaned back in his chair.

"So you wanted to check out the old Mustang, huh? She's a beaut. I keep it in the barn in back so as not to have 'er exposed to the elements. I wasn't sure I'd be able to find it, but I managed to dig out the paperwork for you. Wasn't much, if I'm being honest. But in case you're wondering, I did pay sales tax on it," Horace assured him as he tugged a manila file folder from the kitchen island.

Stephanie's heart kicked into double-time as Ethan opened the folder. She leaned in close, squinting down at the two papers inside. One was a copy of the front side of a canceled check made out to "cash" in the amount of six thousand dollars dated a week after Paul's death, and the other was a title in Horace's name, but nothing identifying the seller that she could see. She pushed back the rush of disappointment and cleared her throat as Ethan took a picture of the title with his phone camera.

"I see the seller isn't named on the title. Is that normal?"

"Actually, when I bought it, the owner said she didn't have the title. It had been destroyed in a fire or some such. I went and just got a bonded title after the fact," Horace explained.

She shot Ethan a questioning glance and he pursed his lips.

"So long as there is a paper trail to prove ownership of the car, the new owner can get a bonded title. Then in a few years, they can apply for a clean title that will allow them to resell the car."

"I'm keeping this baby for my great-grandson. He'll be sixteen in two more years, so didn't make me no difference at the time."

"Horace, do you remember the name of the person that sold you the car?" Ethan asked.

He frowned and nodded slowly. "Rachelle? Or Rachel, maybe? Something like that."

"Was there a man with her?" Ethan asked.

Stephanie held her breath.

"No. She was alone."

"Do you remember what she looked like?" Stephanie pressed, creeping toward the edge of her seat.

Horace took a look around and leaned in to whisper. "Hard to forget. She was a real looker. Blonde, real pretty. Slim build. Had a sad look about her, though. I remember I was thinking I'd bargain her down to fifty-eight hundred, but she seemed so down, I didn't have the heart to do it, so I paid her asking price. The car was worth it."

"Did…did she have a birthmark above her lip that you recall?" Stephanie asked softly.

"She did, matter of fact." Horace's eyes narrowed. "Is she in some kind of trouble? Did I buy a stolen car or something?"

"No, sir. The car is clean and you own it, fair and square. We're just looking for the previous owner in relation to another case, but she's not in any trouble."

Horace's face cleared and he pushed himself to his feet with a groan. "Don't get old, young'uns. Come on out back. I'll show you my baby, if you want to see her."

Stephanie couldn't manage to squeak any words out and was grateful when Ethan took the lead.

"Absolutely."

Rachelle. Or Rachel. Whatever the case, they were one step closer to finding out who Paul's mystery woman was, and it was killing her. Even more so now that they knew the woman had gone to great lengths to get rid of her car without leaving much of a paper trail, and so close to Paul's death. Had she been worried that Stephanie would find out about their affair and tried to cover her tracks? Or was this yet another indication that maybe she and Paul had taken off together? That they'd needed the cash free and clear to make their getaway?

Whatever the case, Stephanie was beside herself. It had gone past closure now. The need to know was an obsession.

She followed the men out the back door to a dilapidated barn and watched in silence as Horace swung the doors open to reveal the yellow vehicle. He was right, it was a real beauty.

Ethan let out a low whistle and nodded. "You were right, you got a great deal on this car."

"Do you mind if I take a picture of it?" Stephanie asked, tugging her phone from her purse.

"Sure, go right ahead."

She snapped the shot and noted she had two missed calls. One from Max and one from Anna.

She made a mental note to check her voicemail when they left and whipped off a text to Max explaining where she was along with the image of the car, requesting that she send it to Lydia for confirmation. Then she slipped her phone back into her purse.

"Horace, thank you so much for your time. If you think of anything else that might help, can you give me a call?" Ethan asked, handing the older man a business card from his pocket.

They said their goodbyes and were back on the road a few minutes later.

For the first five minutes of the drive, they remained silent. She imagined maybe Ethan was giving her time to process her disappointment so as to have a rational discussion about their next move, which was thoughtful of him. But now that she'd been given a crumb, there wasn't enough time in the world to get back to rational. All she wanted to do was get out of this car and get back home so she could do something. Anything to get some answers.

As if on cue, her phone buzzed and she dug it out of her purse again, noting a text reply from Max.

Lydia says that definitely looks like the same car, but she can't be sure. What's going on? Where are you???

She shot back a quick reply, letting Max know she'd be back in a few hours, and then slipped her phone back into her purse.

"My niece sent the picture of the car to Paul's assistant who saw them at the park together. She believes it's the same car." She wrung her hands together and blew out a shaky sigh. "I feel like I'm losing my mind, Ethan. I thought it was a long shot that Horace's car was the same vehicle, but the description of the woman who sold it to him and date of sale are too coincidental. Horace met our girl, and she clearly seemed to be trying to cover her tracks when she sold it. No doubt in my mind. So now what?"

Ethan tightened his grip on the wheel, his gaze trained on the road in front of him. "I agree. That's the car. And I'm not sure what the next move is, but I know it's got to be mine. Between the call activity in the days following Paul's death when his phone should have been at the bottom of the ocean and this new information, I think I've got to officially reopen this case and start going through the proper channels. There will be some red tape involved, which might take a week or two, but from there, things should go very quickly. We've got the VIN from the title, so we should be able to pull the DMV records and get the name of the previous owner fairly quickly. From there, we should be able to track the seller's current whereabouts, so long as she's still in the country."

Stephanie nodded, but inside she felt like she was going to explode. A week or two seemed like eons away. How was she going to cope in the meantime?

She closed her eyes and slumped against the seat, her mind a furious whirl of activity. She stayed like that for the next hour as they drove in silence, the atmosphere so different from that of the ride up. It was so quiet she nearly jumped out of her seat when Ethan's phone trilled halfway through their journey.

He glanced at the number and frowned before hitting the speaker button. "Ethan Jenkins."

"Hello, Detective? It's Horace Breckenridge. Me and Shirley went digging through some old banking paperwork and managed to lay our hands on the canceled check."

Stephanie's eyes went wide as she leaned closer, breathless.

"The signature on the back is pretty legible. The woman's name was Rachel Widener."

The key to unlocking Pandora's box finally had a name. *Rachel Widener.*

Chapter Twenty

"I still can't get my head around it," Anna repeated for the third time. She knew for sure it wasn't improving the situation any, but she couldn't seem to help it. The brother-in-law she'd known and loved was not only kind and generous to a fault, he was also smart. What would have momentarily possessed him to use a traceable method of payment when making purchases for a mistress?

"I know it's hard, Anna. Imagine how I feel. But evidence is evidence. I can't hide my head in the sand if I want to get to the truth," Steph said grimly.

When she'd called Anna to come over after she'd returned from her overnight stay with the sexy detective, Anna had high hopes it was just to gossip about their time together. Instead, she'd been stunned to the tips of her toes to hear all that had occurred in the past two days on the whole Paul front. Now, an hour later as the two of them scrolled through Facebook in search of one Rachel Widener, she was still struggling to come to terms with it all.

She set her laptop aside for a moment and turned to her sister again with a sigh.

"I know it seems like beating a dead horse, but walk me through it. Let's ignore the fact that if Paul did want to cheat, he'd have been sharp enough to pay cash for stuff. The thing that gets me is how out of character it would be. He was a man of such integrity...Remember that time you guys went strawberry picking and the kids ate a handful before you got to the register and Paul insisted on paying five extra dollars for berries just because? Heck, everyone knows kids are going to eat some berries. It's priced into the outrageous per-pound cost, but he wouldn't hear of it, even when the farmer's wife tried to give him the money back. You're expecting me to believe that Paul used a work expense account to pay for a place to slip some floozy the hot beef injection on his lunch hour? That's what you're telling me?"

Stephanie chewed on her already-raw bottom lip and shook her head.

"I don't know what I'm telling you, Anna. But I know that I refuse to let my affection for who I thought Paul was obliterate logic. I won't continue to be made a fool of. I want the truth, once and for all."

Anna stared at her sister again, long and hard. "And what about what Max said? About her friend Tyler seeing Paul out with that woman and them not looking like a couple? You're going to ignore that part?"

Steph drew back and launched herself to her feet. "We have calls, we have receipts, we have multiple eyewitnesses, and we know that Paul lied to me more than once when he was with her!" she shouted, throwing her hands in the air. "I'm supposed to pretend all that means nothing because some kid saw him with the same woman and the two of them managed to not slobber all over one another in public while he was watching for a minute or two?"

Her sister's harsh laugh was anything but funny.

"You can help me find this woman or you can go, Anna. You pick."

Anna nodded slowly and tugged the computer back onto her lap. "I'm not going anywhere. And I'm sorry for pushing you. It's just really hard to imagine Paul—" She broke off, realizing how stupid that must sound to Steph. "If it's hard for me to swallow, I can't even imagine what you're going through. Whatever you need from me, I'm in. You know that."

Steph nodded, swiping away a river of tears.

"I do. And right now what I need to do is find this woman. I want to see what she looks like with my own eyes. Is she married? Does she have kids? I want to know who she is."

"Okay. We've been through every single Rachel Widener on Facebook, and I think it's safe to say if she had an account, she doesn't now or she changed her appearance drastically. Let's move on. You check Insta, and I'll work on LinkedIn."

A half hour later, Anna was sorely wishing she'd switched those tasks around so she didn't have to be the one to break her sister's heart a little more. As she stared into the face of the woman that could only be the Rachel Widener, her stomach twisted into knots. Reports hadn't been wrong. She was lovely. Hell...lovely didn't even cut it. She was a downright stunner. Granted, the picture was a few years old, but unless she'd tripped and fallen into a meat grinder recently, odds were she looked about the same now.

Anna scanned her profile and realized everything was pretty dated. At the time, she was living in Boston, which tracked. She had apparently worked at a place called Lester and Sons Exports and seemingly was unmarried with no children. Anna scrolled through and noted the newest post was dated back to right around the time of Paul's death. As she read it, a chill crept up the back of her neck.

Sometimes life is about taking risks. When it's right, it's right.

After that, it seemed as if Rachel Widener had fallen off the face of the earth.

"Oh my God."

Anna looked up to find Steph leaning over her shoulder, her face bone-white.

"That's...that's her, isn't it?" she whispered, swaying closer.

"I think so," Anna admitted softly. "Steph, I think we should call Ethan and let him know—"

"No. Not yet," Steph shot back. "I just want to try and talk to her before everything gets all sticky. If there are legal ramifications...if Paul faked his own death to be with her or even if he is really dead and she was the last person to see him, having a cop come at her might spook her."

Anna tapped on the keyboard in thought, wishing she could argue with her sister but knowing she was right.

"Well, we don't even know where she lives now or anything. She hasn't posted in years. She could be dead herself, for all we know."

"There's one way to find out," Steph said, rushing across her bedroom floor to snatch her phone from the nightstand.

"And that is?"

"A PI. We have a ton of information on her. It shouldn't be hard for someone to find her."

"Unless she doesn't want to be found," Anna muttered.

Steph glared at her. "Google a highly rated private investigator in the area or I will."

A sense of doom curled around Anna as she did what her sister told her. Best case, the PI wouldn't even be able to start looking for a day or so. By then, Ethan would have gotten his own investigation back in the works and hopefully have some more answers for them.

As much as she wanted her sister to know the truth, she dreaded the pain that would likely come along with it. Sometimes the truth hurt most of all.

"Here's one." She rattled off the telephone number reluctantly, watching as Steph dialed in silence.

Please go to voicemail.

"Hi there, my name is Stephanie Ketterman, and I need to hire a PI to locate someone for me as soon as possible."

Chapter Twenty-One

I can't believe Mick got this built so quickly," Max said in awe as she stared at the bar he had built at the back of her store.

"I can't believe you jumped on my idea so quickly," Tyler said, shaking his head. "When we discussed it a couple of weeks ago, I figured it would take a month minimum, a *few* months conservatively."

"It's a great idea," Max said, then made a conciliatory face. "And then there's the fact I'm desperate and we're about to head into prime tourist season. I couldn't let the opportunity slip by, and when I mentioned it to Mick, he jumped right on it."

"But that was less than two weeks ago, Max," Tyler said. "And this...this is a masterpiece."

Max knew he was right, and she took a bit of silly pride in the fact that the man who had built it was her mother's boyfriend. Now that she'd admitted out loud to Tyler that she was jealous of her mother's business, she'd also admitted to herself that she was jealous of all the time her mother was spending with Mick.

Max loved her mother and wanted nothing but happiness for her, but Cee-cee had always sought her emotional connections with her children since her husband had been emotionally distant. Max was fully aware that there had been a void in her mother's life, a void her children could never fill, and now Mick fit that hole perfectly. Cee-cee couldn't have found a better man if she'd spent years searching. Mick was perfect for her, and more importantly, he made Cee-cee's needs a priority and always made sure she was happy and feeling fulfilled. That had been hard to accept when one, Max was used to her mother's undivided attention, even when it might not have been wanted, and two, Max had been missing that same connection with a man herself.

Max would never begrudge her mother her newfound happiness—Max was thrilled for her. Cee-cee deserved every bit of happiness that came her way, but Max had only recently come to accept that it was okay to feel a bit of jealousy too. As long as she acknowledged its existence and didn't let it interfere with her relationship with her mother.

And Max's pain at not having her own wonderful man had eased since she'd first seen Tyler in the bar. They'd only been out a few times, but she had an inkling that he might be her own Mick.

She realized it was too soon to truly know something like that, but Aunt Stephanie had told her and Sarah that sometimes that was how love struck. Sometimes it was like a tiny seed that grew slowly over time, spreading out deep, thick roots to help that love hold on in the storms life threw at you. But other times, you knew in an instant—he's the one for me.

"That's how I felt when I met your daddy," Aunt Stephanie had said to a middle-school-aged Sarah, then turned to Max. "Your uncle Paul. I took one look at him and I knew—he was the one for me."

It was strange, because Max had known Tyler all through high school and never once had that thought entered her mind, but seeing him in the bar...she'd known. This was the man she was going to spend the rest of her life with.

It was equally exciting and terrifying.

That was part of the reason she'd jumped on the bar idea so quickly. It could get messy becoming business partners with someone she was in a romantic entanglement with, but why not eagerly say yes to a business commitment when she foresaw an even longer commitment to him in her future? Especially when it entwined so well with his own dreams and passions? She was eager to embark on all of it...but right now, they needed to focus on saving her business.

And Tyler was helping her do it.

The bar Mick built was beautiful, and being Mick, he'd made sure the design fit the eclectic look of the store with its one wall of exposed brick, the worn, weathered original wood floor, and the original woodwork. When Mick had helped Max freshen up the space before she'd opened, he quizzed her on her own personal style. While he'd kept a lot of the character of the place—and stripped out some 1990s nonsense the previous renter had installed—he'd also incorporated contemporary pieces such as light fixtures and bookshelves.

Max had never doubted that Mick could come through, but the bar had far exceeded her expectations. There wasn't a lot of room in the back, so he'd found a pair of short, matching antique fireplace mantels and set them end to end over a piece of wood for the front of the bar, making the counter taller in the front, and shorter in the back for whomever tended the bar. He'd put cabinets along the back wall, and several vintage mirrors above them, with a long rack spanning between two tall cabinets that held wine refrigerators—both of which were Tyler's contribution to the building project. Between Tyler's bar experience and Mick's construction and designer's eye, they'd come up with the perfect plan.

Max still couldn't believe they'd done it in less than two weeks.

And now she and Tyler were waiting on her mother and her aunt Anna to show up to help them unpack all the glasses and utensils. But first would be dinner.

As if on cue, the door jingled behind them and Max turned to see her mother and her aunt Anna walking in, Anna carrying a large takeout bag from Giovanni's.

"We're here and ready to be put to work!" Anna called out as she blew in like a Nor'easter. "But not until after I eat all these beautiful carbs."

Cee-cee followed behind, shutting the door and then stooping to pick up a napkin Anna had dropped. "Sorry we're late. We got detained at Giovanni's."

"Uh, more like you were trying to spy on Aunt Steph on the pier," Max said with her hands on her hips and a raised brow. "You don't fool me for a second."

Her aunt Stephanie was supposed to help them until she'd gotten a mind-blowing email that morning that changed her plans.

Cee-cee pinched her lips together, but Anna had never been shy about her nosiness. She set the takeout bag on the large coffee table in the middle of the room.

"I may have finally agreed about her going to the meeting, and I may have agreed to not watch from the distance, but I can't help it if Giovanni's is slow with their takeout orders and they let me look at the view out their windows."

"The view of the pier," Cee-cee said with a scowl. "And we showed up ten minutes early. You gave them the wrong pickup time."

"I can't help it if I have chemo brain," Anna said with a grin. "And she wasn't even there. How are we supposed to know when they are meeting if she won't even tell us? What kind of sister is that?"

"One who doesn't want to be spied on," Cee-cee said dryly.

Her mother had a point. If Max were meeting her husband's potential mistress, she wouldn't want her family watching either. How humiliating.

Anna headed toward the bar, apparently ready to change the topic. "Okay, wine boy, hook me up. What goes with fettuccine?"

Tyler laughed and headed to the white wine fridge. "For you, Anna, I recommend a full-bodied white wine. I have a nice Pinot Bianco that would go well with alfredo sauce."

"Hey!" Anna protested. "Watch who you're calling full-bodied!"

A look of horror washed over Tyler's face, and Max was about to tell him her aunt was teasing when Anna burst out laughing.

"The look on your face!" Anna said, pointing at him.

"My sister has her warped sense of humor," Cee-cee said, shedding her light jacket and laying it neatly over the back of a chair. "But she has the right idea about the wine. I'm a bundle of nerves waiting for Steph to tell us what happens. I definitely need a drink. I'm having penne pasta with vodka sauce. What would you pair with that?"

"For you, Cee-cee, I have a Sangiovese from Napa Valley. It has a great fruity overtone, and the acidity pairs nicely with the vodka sauce," Tyler said as he grabbed two freshly washed white wine glasses out of a box and set them on the counter, then grabbed two red wine glasses.

"I feel like we finally got some class in this family," Anna said with a nod as she approached the bar, looking it over. "And Mick's a nice touch too. Look what that man can do with his hands." Then she winked at Cee-cee, who blushed profusely.

"Anna!"

Max just shook her head and laughed, then glanced over at Tyler to gauge his reaction.

Tyler was grinning ear to ear, not that Max had expected any less. He was used to dealing with characters at his father's bar. Still, dealing with them in your girlfriend's extended family was another situation altogether.

"Max told me about Stephanie's meeting," Tyler said as he opened a bottle of white wine first. "I can't believe how this has all unfolded."

Max couldn't believe it herself.

Nearly two weeks ago, her aunt had gone with Detective Jenkins to look at a car they thought might have belonged to the woman her uncle Paul had been meeting before his death. Stephanie had gotten the woman's name—Rachel Widener—and had found a PI in Boston, Rachel's last known location, to track her down.

But hiring a PI had been more of an issue than Steph had expected. She'd discovered most PIs won't take a case to locate someone unless the client agrees that while the person might be found, the PI won't give the client the person's information without their consent.

"What mistress is going to consent to meeting her dead lover's wife?" Steph had scoffed. So she'd spent several days calling over a dozen private investigators, all of whom agreed with the first investigator she'd spoken to, saying the contract protected potential victims from stalkers and domestic violence abusers. And even if Steph had agreed to contract with them, most of the investigators couldn't fit her into their schedule for another week.

So Stephanie had gone with the first investigator she'd contacted, who hadn't gotten to her case until a few days before. She was shocked when the investigator called her a day later and said that he'd contacted Ms. Widener, and that she was undecided as to whether she wanted to have contact with Stephanie. The PI had left all of Steph's contact information with Rachel and told her that all she could do was hope and wait.

Steph had been heartbroken and sure that was the last she'd hear from Rachel, but to her surprise, Rachel had emailed her that morning, asking Steph to meet her at the Bluebird Bay Pier.

Max's mother had protested the alone part, but Steph had insisted, saying that she and Detective Jenkins had it covered.

So now all they could do was wait, but waiting wasn't Anna's strong suit.

"What do you say we have a drink, then head down to Gabe's fishing boat and check it out?" Anna said as Tyler handed her a glass of wine. She took a sip, then added, "Or maybe a drink or two. This is really good."

Tyler beamed. "Wait until you try it with the pasta."

"We're not going to check out my brother's boat," Max said. "We're going to respect Aunt Steph's request for privacy."

"Even if it kills us," Cee-cee said as she took the glass Tyler offered her.

"Or kills Steph," Anna said.

Cee-cee turned on her in an instant. "Not funny, Anna."

Anna's face was somber. "I'm not *being* funny. What if this Rachel Widener is a spurned lover who plans to take out the wife in revenge?"

"Revenge for what?" Max asked. "You've been watching too many Lifetime movies, Aunt Anna. Time to change back to Animal Planet."

Anna scowled. "They have too many dang law enforcement shows these days. If I want to watch people get arrested, I'll find a *Cops* marathon and see the good stuff."

"Aunt Stephanie's going to be fine," Max assured them all.

She only hoped she was right.

Chapter Twenty-Two

Stephanie couldn't believe any of this.

Months ago, she couldn't believe that her husband would have an affair.

Weeks ago, she couldn't believe he'd had a secret lover.

Days ago, she couldn't believe that she'd tracked down his lover and that she couldn't make contact with her.

This morning, she couldn't believe when she saw the email in her inbox titled, *Okay, I'll meet you but . . .*

Stephanie had been on a roller coaster of emotions the last three years, but the last month or so had been the absolute worst.

But now she hoped to get her answers. The ones she so desperately needed so she could put a close on her life with Paul and move on to the next phase. A phase that likely wouldn't include Ethan Jenkins. Not after what Bryan had shared with her.

But she couldn't consider a potential future with *anyone* when she was so firmly stuck in her past with Paul. She needed Rachel Widener to show tonight. She needed her to be forthcoming with her answers, and then she needed to let it go—easier said than done, but she was sure she'd figure out how with the help of her therapist.

Pop was settled with the night nurse and Todd was in the study, researching veterinary client programs, which left Steph to sit in her kitchen, stewing.

She poured herself a small glass of wine to try to settle her nerves, then checked her phone one more time. Rachel had said she'd text Stephanie when she'd arrived, but it was nearly eight and she still hadn't texted.

Had she changed her mind? Should Steph text her and make sure it was still on? Did she have the right phone number?

Steph opened her email app and reread the email Rachel had sent.

I've decided to meet you, but you have to be alone. This is too embarrassing to discuss in front of your friends or family. I can meet you tonight on the docks at Bluebird Bay Pier. I'll text you when I'm close.

R

Steph had emailed immediately, agreeing to Rachel's terms and including her cell phone number in case Rachel had misplaced it, which was highly unlikely since she'd emailed.

But it occurred to Stephanie that she couldn't text the woman even if she wanted to. Rachel had her number, but Steph didn't have hers.

Several times throughout the day she'd considered emailing Rachel and calling the whole thing off. Steph was afraid of the answers she would get. How could she listen to another woman talk about their love for one another? How they'd slipped off for rendezvous right under her nose? How could she bear the humiliation and the pain?

Bryan had called her in the morning, asking if she had any updates. She told him about the email, and he'd encouraged her to go through with it.

"You can finally get the answers you're looking for," he'd said. "I can go with you if you like. For support."

"That's okay," she'd told him. "I need to do this on my own."

"Well, if you decide to take someone, please call me. I'm a good third-party, emotionally neutral person."

"Thanks," she'd said but left it at that, not wanting to encourage him after the discussion they'd had a couple of days before.

He'd called and asked her to meet him for coffee, telling her he had something important to discuss.

When they'd met, he made some idle chitchat about his dog and Todd before Steph said, "Bryan, I'm on pins and needles here. What did you have to tell me that's important?"

He squirmed. "Are you still seeing that police detective?"

"Ethan?" she'd asked in surprise. "Why?"

"What do you know about this guy?" he'd asked.

"Not much, but that's why we're dating, Bryan," she'd said with a laugh. "We're getting to know each other."

He'd frowned. "But is he safe?"

"He's a police detective," she'd said, grinning at his protectiveness. "How much safer can you get?"

"Did you know that a lot of cops are domestic abusers? And that they get away with it because of that band of brotherhood, or whatever they call it," he said, getting flustered. "I don't want you to get hurt, Stephanie." The look in his eyes had suggested he was holding something back.

His concern had caught her by surprise. "Do you know something I don't?"

He shifted in his seat, clearly uncomfortable. "You know he's divorced, right? Did he tell you why?"

Her back stiffened. "I'm not sure that's relevant."

"It is if his wife was in the ER with bruises on her face and arms days before she left him."

Her heart stopped and she stared at him in disbelief. "*What?*"

Grimacing, he leaned closer and lowered his voice. "Stephanie, you know I'm not one to gossip, but what I heard yesterday alarmed me. That's why I asked you to meet me. So we could discuss it in person."

"Go on," she said with a shaky breath.

"Lydia was asking about you the other day since she knows we've been in contact recently, and I told her that you were seeing Detective Jenkins. One of the girls in the office overheard us and told us about his history with his wife. And a girlfriend after his divorce. ER visits. Black eyes. Apparently, he comes across as a really great guy, but get him drunk and angry . . ." Bryan let the insinuation hang in the air for several seconds before he covered Steph's hand with his own. "I'm so sorry, Stephanie."

She'd stared at him in horror. How could this be true? How had she missed the signs? But then, she'd missed the signs that her husband was having an affair, so her judgment was obviously not to be trusted. "Thank you, Bryan. Thank you for going out of your way to protect me."

"I care about you, Steph," he'd said with more warmth in his voice than she was used to hearing, and she realized his hand was still covering hers. "I care about you a lot."

Her brain tried to absorb what he'd just said, but it was one shock too many.

"You're a beautiful woman, Stephanie Ketterman," he'd said, his thumb stroking the back of her hand. "I've been giving you space, letting you grieve before I told you that I'm interested in you. And then you slipped away to another man. But this warning isn't me with bitter grapes. I want you to be happy, Steph, whether that's with me or with someone else, but *please*, I'm begging you, stay far away from Ethan Jenkins because he's dangerous."

She'd taken off soon after that, her head a mess of emotions. She already had doubts about Paul. She didn't need doubts about Ethan too. She wasn't going to buy into rumors and conjecture without at least talking to him, but Bryan's news had been too much to deal with. She could only handle one crisis at a time, and she'd needed to deal with Paul first, then Ethan.

He could wait.

So she'd canceled their date that night and she'd been screening his calls. She liked him too much and she was worried that if he really was an abuser that her psyche was in a state that would permit him to gaslight her. She'd vowed to herself not to see him again until she talked to Dr. Yang and get her take on the situation.

But now Stephanie felt guilty for telling her sisters that she had Ethan for backup tonight, going so far as to let them—more like Anna—hypothesize what that meant and how much surveillance Ethan would be doing and then not bothering to correct her.

The truth was Ethan had no idea this meeting was even taking place.

Her phone buzzed with a text and her heart leapt into her throat. It was from Ethan.

Steph, if I've offended you somehow, I'm truly sorry. Can we please talk about it?

Ethan didn't deserve to be ghosted, and she really did want to talk to him and get his side of the story, but not now. Not tonight.

She took another sip of her wine.

Her phone started to ring and she wasn't sure whether to be relieved or annoyed that it was Bryan.

"Have you heard from her yet?" he asked as soon as she answered.

"No. Nothing." She poured herself more wine and took a sip.

"Do you think she chickened out?"

She pushed out a sigh. "I'm not sure, but it crossed my mind. It's after eight."

He paused, then said, "I can come sit with you if you like. Even drive you to the dock if she does end up texting you. I don't think you should do this alone."

She didn't want to do this alone either, and she'd plowed through one glass of wine and had started another. She probably shouldn't be driving, so she considered his offer, then decided against it. "I appreciate the offer, Bryan, you have no idea, but I need to do this alone, and I'll likely just take an Uber since I'm on my second glass of wine. But," she added, feeling disheartened, "I doubt it will be an issue. She's a no-show."

"Maybe we could find her ourselves," Bryan suggested. "Go to Boston and start searching. If the PI found her in a day, then surely we can find her too."

"Maybe," Steph said, feeling dejected. "But I can't think about it right now."

"Have another glass of wine. Get a good night's sleep, and we can discuss it in the morning," Bryan said.

"Thanks. I'll talk to you tomorrow."

Stephanie sat at the kitchen counter, mulling over their call as she finished her glass. She was about to pour another one when her phone dinged with a text.

Meet me at the docks in twenty minutes. Slip 37. Come alone. I'll give you until 9 and if you don't show, I'm leaving.

Steph quickly glanced at the time on her phone. 8:38. That didn't give her much time.

She quickly ordered an Uber and the app told her the car was five minutes away. She rinsed out her glass and loaded it into the dishwasher, recorked the wine and put it back in the fridge, then wiped off the counter and went out the kitchen door to the side of the house. If Todd or Pop saw her go out the front door, she didn't want to have to come up with an explanation about where she was going and why she wasn't driving.

The Uber was a few minutes late, making her even more nervous. What if Rachel left before Steph got there?

The driver tried to make small talk, but she quickly realized that Steph wasn't in a chatty mood. Steph was so antsy, she thought she was going to implode. Especially since she was running behind.

As soon as the car stopped at the curb, Stephanie thanked the driver, then bolted out the door, checking the time—8:57.

A fog had rolled in, partially obscuring the docks, and it had begun to rain, but she raced for them anyway, realizing that she was practically running to Paul's mistress. What had happened to her pride? What had happened to *her*? She was a dignified, professional woman and her life was falling to shit.

She got halfway down the dock and came to an abrupt halt.

What was she doing? Chasing a ghost. A shadow. She'd been happy in her life with Paul. Maybe she needed to let go of everything she'd found out about her husband after his death and fall back on the good times. She'd seen love in his eyes nearly every day of her life for over thirty years. She'd seen it the morning that he'd drowned as he kissed her in the bathroom, slow and lazy as though they had their whole lives to revel in each other's arms. The way he'd cajoled her to take off work and spend the day with him on the boat. There was no faking that. He'd loved her. Loved her with his entire being. If he'd had a fling with another woman, it had been meaningless, because he'd come home to her every night. Maybe that could be enough for her to live with. To let this obsession go.

This was her choice, and it had been all along. She could accept that he was human and had made a mistake, and honor his memory the way she'd honored him in life, or she could plunge deeper into this pit of torment that only provided more and more pain instead of the relief she so desperately needed.

That had been her choice all along.

She was choosing Paul.

She was choosing the happy memories of her husband. The laughter and the joy. The quiet, intimate moments where they shared their lives and their hearts. There was no faking that. Those moments had been real, and she chose to remember those. With Dr. Yang's help, she could move on from this. She'd find her way out of this anguish, but it meant turning around and walking away.

So she did.

Or she started to, until she saw a figure in the mist further down the pier, a man with an amazingly similar profile to Paul's.

Had his ghost come to give her his blessing? Or was he really alive and he'd come with Rachel to tell her to let him go? No, she refused to believe that one, not after her choice.

The figure seemed to watch her for a moment, then headed into the fog.

"Paul?" she whispered to herself, and she began to follow without giving it conscious thought. It briefly occurred to her that she was tipsy enough that it might not be a good idea for her to be walking on the gently moving docks, but now that she'd begun to follow the figure, she couldn't bring herself to stop. If it was Paul's ghost, or more likely an alcohol-induced psychotic break, she was going to tell him she forgave him for his past sins and give him—and herself—permission to move on.

The figure stopped and she slowly approached it.

"Hello?" she said. It felt too foolish to call him by name.

The man turned and she let out a gasp when she saw that it was Bryan.

Shaking her head and nearly falling over from the swaying of the dock and her off-kilter equilibrium, she said, "Bryan. What are you doing here? I told you I needed to do this by myself . . ."

A condescending look washed over his face as he held up a gun and pointed it straight at her chest. "Why couldn't you have just left it alone, Steph?"

Chapter Twenty-Three

Cee-cee was exhausted. She, Anna, and Max had been unboxing more types of glasses than she knew existed, while Tyler had been arranging the wine bottles in the wine refrigerators and in the cabinet. Tyler had convinced the landlord into giving him access to the basement, and he had constructed his own wine racks to store his stock.

Petey called around nine and asked Tyler to come handle a situation at the bar.

"I hate to leave, but I'll come back tomorrow morning and finish the basement," he said to Max.

"We're fine," she said, smiling up at him. "I'll see you tomorrow."

He gave her a lingering kiss goodbye, and a long look that told Cee-cee that the man was crazy about her daughter. She wasn't sure if that made her feel better about the financial situation or worse.

When Tyler left, Cee-cee turned to her daughter. "Are you sure you should be spending this much money?"

A fire flashed in Max's eyes, so Cee-cee held up her hand. "I'm sorry. It's your money. Your business. It's just that you're already stretched thin financially." She gave Max an apologetic smile. "You're my only daughter and I love you. I'm worried, is all, but feel free to tell me to butt out."

Max smiled and gave her mother a tight hug. "I love you, Mom, and I love that you're worried about me. But you don't need to be. Tyler's so excited about this project and believes in it so much that he's funded nearly one hundred percent of it. In fact, he's already talking to the landlord about expanding into the next space."

Cee-cee frowned. Max wasn't breaking even with the space she had, and now she was talking about expanding? This had disaster written all over it.

Max gave her a reassuring smile and rubbed the frown lines on Cee-cee's forehead. "Don't worry, Mom. One way or the other, I'll be okay."

"But this seems more like Tyler's venture than yours, and it all just happened so fast."

"I know it seems that way, but for the first time in a long time, I'm really excited about the bookstore, and I think it's a great idea. I like working with Tyler. He's enthusiastic and supportive, and he makes me happy."

"But you barely know him, Max."

"That's not true," Max said. "We knew each other from school, but let's talk about what's really bothering you. It's Aunt Steph, isn't it?"

Cee-cee slumped and nodded, wishing she could get rid of the knot in her stomach. "I tried texting her and calling her and her phone is turned off."

"What?" Anna screeched. "She promised me she would leave it on. I tried texting her and haven't gotten a response either. Maybe that woman didn't show up and she's wallowing alone."

"Or maybe she did and she didn't like what she heard," Cee-cee said, wincing.

"That seems like a distinct possibility," Max said. "Maybe we should call Detective Jenkins."

"Good idea," Anna said.

Cee-cee grabbed her cell phone off the counter and pulled up the officer's number.

"Detective Jenkins," he said when he answered.

"Detective, this is Cee-cee Burrows. Stephanie's sister."

Max snatched the phone from her mother's hand and put the phone on speaker.

"I'm so glad you called. I've actually been trying to reach her," he said. "I called her again this afternoon to tell her I needed to talk to her about something important, but she never returned my call."

Cee-cee's mouth dropped open as her pulse kicked up a notch. "What?"

"She hasn't taken my calls all week," he said. "And I honestly have no idea why she's ignoring me, but that's her prerogative. I just know she's been desperate to get more information on the case and I finally have some for her."

Cee-cee looked at Anna in bewilderment.

"If you haven't talked to Stephanie all week," Anna said, "then why did she say you were going to be with her tonight?"

"She said I was with her tonight?" he asked, then quickly added, "Not that I don't want to be with her—I do—it's just that we didn't have plans."

"She lied to us," Anna hissed, her eyes wide.

It was so unlike her that Cee-cee didn't believe it. Stephanie *never* lied. What on earth was going on?

"Why do I feel like I'm missing something?" the detective asked, sounding anxious.

"Detective Jenkins," Cee-cee said in a calm voice that belied her rising fear. "Stephanie told us she was meeting with Rachel Widener tonight and that you knew about and approved the meeting."

"Are you certain?" he asked. "That's why I've been trying to get ahold of Stephanie. I was down in Boston today interviewing Ms. Widener. She contacted her local police precinct and told them she had information about Paul's death. I went there to interview *her*. She refused to come to Bluebird." He paused, then said, "Where are you three? I'm coming to you."

"At my bookstore," Max said, worry filling her eyes. "At the corner of—"

"I know where it is," he said. "Hang tight. I'll be right there." Then he hung up.

Cee-cee's head swam as she turned to Max in confusion. "I don't understand."

Max wrapped her arm around her mother's back and led her to the sofa. "Why don't you come sit down? You too, Aunt Anna."

But while Cee-cee felt like the floor had fallen out from underneath her, Anna looked like she was spoiling for a fight.

"Why would she lie to us?" Anna demanded.

"I don't know," Cee-cee said as she sat down. "Was she really meeting her?"

"I know a way to find out," Max said as she pulled out her phone and placed a call. "Todd," she said, starting to pace. "It's Max. Is your mom home?" After a moment, she asked, "Will you see if she's there anyway? She's not answering any of our calls or texts." She lowered her phone and directed her response to Cee-cee and Anna. "He says her car is there and he's going to look for her in the house."

"So she never went to the pier," Anna said with a sigh of relief. "That's good. It's pouring out now, and if she's not herself, upset and out there in the rain...rogue waves can be unpredictable."

Max held up her hand as she listened to her phone. "You're sure she's not there?" She paused. "Okay. Yeah, she told my mom and Aunt Anna she was supposed to meet that woman tonight at the docks, you know, the one your father supposedly met up with before his death." She made a face. "We're at my bookstore and Detective Jenkins is headed over. Why don't you come over too? Detective Jenkins says he went to Boston to meet Rachel Widener there today. He's going to tell us what she said, and we're going to try to figure out where your mom is. Okay. We'll see you then." When she hung up, she glanced at her mother. "Todd's coming over."

"That's probably a good idea. I have a very bad feeling about all of this." Cee-cee could feel it in her bones. Something was very wrong.

Todd pulled up just as Ethan Jenkins was walking through the shop's front door, and raced in behind him.

"Todd," the detective said with a nod of his head.

"I hope you can help us find my mother, Detective Jenkins," Todd said, his voice tight. "Because she's missing and her car is at home."

"Call me Ethan," the older man said, placing his hand on Todd's upper arm. "And trust me, I'm going to do everything in my power to help."

Cee-cee, Max, and Todd sat down on the sofa, but Anna paced behind them, obviously needing to keep moving. She never had been a *sit-around-and-wait* kind of woman. Ethan stood in front of them, his face drawn. "As I mentioned to Cee-cee earlier on the phone, I went down to

Boston to speak to Rachel Widener today. Right out of the gate, I should let you all know that Paul Ketterman almost certainly didn't fake his own death, and he was not having an affair."

The group let out a collective gasp of bittersweet relief, but Anna asked, "How can you be sure? What if Rachel was just lying to you and covering her butt?"

"Because Ms. Widener was very convincing...*and* because she's a lesbian," he added. "She laughed in my face when I asked her if they had been having an affair. She says she's been with the same partner for four years. However, her partner was also unaware that Ms. Widener had been meeting Paul. The two kept it secret, thus their clandestine meetings."

"Why?" Todd asked, clearly bewildered. "What were they meeting about?"

"Rachel Widener is a whistle-blower. She worked for Haskell and Martin, the accounting firm in Portland in charge of auditing the books for Perkins and Ketterman. One of Bryan Perkins' clients requested an audit of their books, so he hired Haskell and Martin to review them. Ms. Widener became aware of the situation when her boss asked her to review a case and accidently gave her access to the wrong file—Bryan's case. She'd only had it for a few minutes, but her boss quickly realized his mistake and tried to cover his butt, telling her to ignore and delete the first file and focus on the second that he'd just sent. Deleting a file went against protocol, so naturally the file piqued her interest and she copied it to a flash drive before deleting it, then took it home and began to study it that night. She soon realized the client's books had been altered. Ms. Widener was certain that Bryan Perkins had done the altering, and that her boss was covering for him. However, she was young and only a few years out of school and unsure what to do. She'd met Paul before at a conference and he'd seemed kind and honest, so she took a chance and called him."

"I can't even imagine what I would have done if I'd found myself in a situation like that," Max said. "I can't imagine how scared she must have been, but I know I would have turned to Uncle Paul too."

Todd wrapped an arm around her back and leaned his head into hers. "Dad loved you, Max. He was so proud that you became an accountant like him. You would have done the right thing."

A lump filled Cee-cee's throat. "Please continue, Detective."

Ethan gave them an understanding look, then continued, "After Ms. Widener showed him what she'd found, he asked her to keep an eye out for other files from their office. He knew of three other client files going for an audit—surprisingly initiated by Bryan himself, not the clients. Likely to cover himself since Paul had become aware that a few of Bryan's clients were unhappy. He was probably trying to prove that everything was okay, but Paul began to suspect Bryan Perkins was skimming off the top."

Todd shook his head, his face red and his eyes filled with tears. "I can't believe it. Bryan was there for us after dad's death. He took me to Portland to a Mariners game when I was home for Christmas break. He said he knew how much I loved hockey and that Dad took me to a game when I came home for the holidays."

Ethan gave him a sympathetic look, then said, "Ms. Widener and Paul met the morning of his death. She had finished compiling the results of her own audit, and they were planning how to present the information to the police. Paul volunteered to come to us and leave her name completely out of it. He'd tell them he stumbled upon it himself. Ms. Widener waited to hear about the results of the meeting, but a few days passed, and nothing. She tried to call and got voicemail. She found out about Paul's disappearance at sea and presumed death days later. She realized someone must have killed Paul to keep him from exposing their embezzlement. Believing she could be next, if they caught on to her involvement, she quit her job, sold just about everything she owned, and moved within two weeks. Her girlfriend was in Boston, so she moved in with her and started over—new life, new career, new everything. Anything and everything she could do to distance herself from Paul, Haskell and Martin, and Bryan Perkins."

Tears flooded Cee-cee's eyes as she asked, "Do you think Bryan Perkins killed Paul?"

The detective gave her a solemn look. "He's definitely a suspect."

"Cut the police-speak," Todd snapped as he jumped to his feet, his hands clenched at his sides. "Do you think he did it or not?"

"Yeah," Ethan conceded, his shoulders slumping. "I think he's responsible."

"Stephanie's in trouble," Anna said, her voice rising. "She's been in contact with Bryan all week. In fact, the deeper she got into investigating the woman Paul had been meeting, the more interested Bryan became. I know he's been on pins and needles while Steph waited to find out if Rachel would be willing to talk to her. She surely told him that Rachel wanted to meet her on the docks tonight."

"And Rachel told her she had to be alone or the meeting was off," Anna said. "Steph wouldn't let us come. She didn't even know *when* or exactly where on the pier she was supposed to meet her. She was to wait for a text."

"Rachel wasn't meeting Stephanie tonight," Ethan said. "She made it very clear she wanted to give me her statement and be done with the entire thing. She never wants to see Bluebird Bay again."

"Then who was Stephanie meeting and why was she meeting them at the docks?" Cee-cee asked, already knowing the answer deep in her bones.

"Bryan Perkins," Todd said, sounding gutted.

Fear filled Ethan's eyes and he headed for the door, saying, "I'm going to find her."

The group watched him leave, then stared at each other for a beat.

Anna held her hands out at her sides. "If you all plan on sitting here playing tiddlywinks while my sister's missing, you go for it, but I'm going to those docks to find her."

Cee-cee jumped up. "I'm coming with you."

"Don't you dare consider leaving me out of this," Todd said through clenched teeth. "When I get my hands on that man . . ."

They were close enough to the pier that it was quicker to sprint through the sheets of rain and whipping winds than it was to drive and park. Ethan's car was parked at the curb and he was talking to someone on the phone when they got there. They rushed right past him and started down the dock.

"Hey!" Ethan called after them. "Stay off the docks! They're unstable in this weather, and that's a potential crime scene! I already went down and she's not there!"

None of them listened, instead entering the thin fog, searching for any sign of Stephanie. Max and Todd raced ahead while Cee-cee and Anna searched the water between the boats, calling out her name.

"Mom!" Max cried out several feet ahead. "I found her phone!"

Cee-cee and the rest hurried over, the sisters confirming her find.

"Bryan's boat is missing," Todd said, his voice shaking. "I think he took my mom out to sea."

Max snatched her own phone out of her pocket. "I'm calling Gabe."

Cee-cee nodded, feeling close to passing out. They weren't helpless. Gabe had a boat. They'd find her sister.

Chapter Twenty-Four

When her eyes finally opened, Stephanie's whole world was topsy-turvy and her stomach lurched.

She swallowed hard, her tongue feeling thick in her mouth as she tried to remember where she was and what had happened. Last thing she recalled was heading over to the pier to meet Rachel and—

Bryan. She sat up as far as the ropes tying her in place would allow, the throbbing in her head painful enough to make her gasp. That bastard had pistol-whipped her. And judging by the rolling and pitching motion of the wooden floor under her bottom, he'd dragged her onto his boat and out to sea.

She tugged against her restraints as she tried to gather her scattered thoughts and think through the pain, but a low, menacing voice cut in.

"Don't bother. Those knots aren't going to budge, and even if you managed to get free, there's nowhere to go. We're five nautical miles out in the middle of the Atlantic."

She turned her head slowly to find Bryan sitting on a stool in the galley a few yards away, calmly drinking from a steaming mug, like they were old pals discussing the weather.

But the icy gleam in his eye and the chill in his voice told another story.

The story of a man with no conscience.

"Paul didn't die in a tragic accident. You killed him," she managed, unable to mask her horror and fury.

He nodded and shrugged, not even bothering to deny it.

But why?

"I didn't kill him. I just gave him something to make him fall asleep and then rigged his boat. Mother Nature did the rest. If she hadn't, I'd have found the guts to kill him, though. He was poking his nose in places he shouldn't have been," he said, answering her unspoken question. "Just like you were." He shook his head slowly and set his mug down with a clack. "Don't look at me like that!" he snapped, the sudden fire in his eyes twice as terrifying as the ice had been. "I loved him, Stephanie. And I love you too, but you have to understand. I had to protect myself. If they found out I'd been skimming, they'd have taken everything from me. Even if I only did a few years in a white-collar prison, I'd lose my house, my boat, my country club membership, my friends...I'd never work again. And how could I even face Sandra and my son?" He raked a hand through his hair as he pushed himself to his feet. "All he had to do was mind his own damned business, but nooo!"

Bryan began to pace and Stephanie found it hard to believe she'd never seen a hint of this person in all the years she'd known him. A twisted, broken individual on the verge of snapping. Had Paul been blind to it too? Had he trusted Bryan until the very end?

"So this was about money?" she spat, her whole body trembling now. "You were stealing and Paul figured it out, so you what? Pretended you wanted to have some heart-to-heart with him out on the boat and were going to turn yourself in?"

"I earned that money!" Bryan shot back, wild eyes blazing. "I busted my butt, schmoozing all the clients, spending countless hours getting new business, sacrificing my own marriage so Paul could spend weekends and evenings home with his precious family. And what did it get me? A big fat divorce and half of everything I did earn being taken from me by my bitch of an ex! What was I supposed to do, Stephanie?"

"Paul was happy with the success of the business as it was. He'd always wanted it to be a hands-on firm, not some big, faceless conglomerate. You were both doing very well by any standard. You didn't need more clients. For Pete's sake, he loved you like a brother, Bryan," she said, now weeping as it all sank in for real. "He was almost ready to retire, and you'd have had it all."

Bryan drew back at that, his mouth opening and closing wordlessly, and for a second, she wondered if she might have gotten through to the monster, but then he sneered at her.

"Always the fricking martyr. Paul's just sooo fabulous. What a great guy. Well, now he gets to be the martyr for real, doesn't he?"

She still couldn't quite accept it all. Her husband had been murdered for something he'd have gladly handed over if he'd been asked. The tragedy of that struck her deep in the heart as she tried to think clearly.

Paul was dead, but she wasn't. Everything they'd built together, everything they had...their life, their home, their children...it was all just on the shore, awaiting her return.

Images of her kids flickered through her mind and she sucked in a shuddering breath. She would not let her daughter get married without one of her parents there to share that joy with her.

The kids needed her. Cee-cee, Anna, and Pop needed her. And she needed to explain to Ethan why she'd pulled away...

But the only way to do any of that was to keep Bryan talking until someone realized she was missing. Her sisters had to realize by now. They were all so close, and Stephanie knew for sure Anna wouldn't have been able to quell her curiosity long enough to keep herself from trying to get in touch. But would they be able to piece it together? The more time she gave them to try, the better. And if worse came to worst, she'd use that time to try and free herself. If it came down to a physical battle, she'd fare much better if she wasn't tied up. She began worrying the knots again with her fingertips as she kept her gaze locked on Bryan.

"So was it all lies, then? About the hotel rooms and the flowers? Ethan beating his wife? And what about Rachel Widener? Did you kill her too?"

"Not yet. Truth be told, I'm not too worried about her. She didn't contact you back when you reached out to her, and your dumb cop boyfriend hasn't been coming around me asking questions, so something tells me Rachel gets it. She'll do what she chose to do when Paul died. Hide her head in the sand and be glad she was spared. If I'm wrong, it won't matter. I'll be out of the country by the time they're able to verify anything she has to say. You were the one who just wouldn't stop pushing. So you see, it's not my fault, Stephanie. I'm just doing what I have to in order to survive."

She was about to reply when the boat pitched hard to the left and sent Bryan stumbling. He grabbed onto the wall for purchase and scowled at her.

"I chose tonight on account of the rough seas, knowing it would make it hard for anyone to come looking even if they did figure it out, but the winds are really picking up now. I'd love to keep you around a little while longer. I know you think I'm a horrible person, but I don't enjoy killing, Stephanie. I just enjoy the concept of prison and being poor a little less." With that, he inched closer, pulling the gun he'd struck her with from his waistband.

Panic rushed in as Stephanie tried to think of more ways to stall.

"Do you honestly think you're going to get away with this twice?" she demanded, tugging more feverishly at the ropes behind her back. "That no one will think it's strange that hometown sweethearts, a husband and wife with no criminal past, both wind up missing and presumed dead under suspicious circumstances? I got to the docks via Uber, Bryan. Half a dozen people were aware of where I was going, not to mention the email you sent me from the fake account you set up for Rachel. You don't think they'll be able to track that?"

He let out a harsh laugh and shrugged. "They will find it leads to a burner phone. And everyone you knew watched you spiraling out of control into this depression since Paul died. Do you honestly think it's out of the realm of possibility that you threw yourself into the sea to join him?"

Her throat went bone-dry. "My family will never believe that."

"They don't need to. Only the cops do. And without a body, how do you think they're going to charge anyone with murder? It's nearly impossible. Plus, I'll have plenty of time to empty my accounts and skip out if any of that comes to pass. Now stop trying to buy time. This party is over."

211

He closed the distance between them and Stephanie said a silent prayer under her breath as she finally worked one of the knots binding her hands loose. She still didn't have full use of her arms, but if she could just get a moment, she could make use of her yoga training and shimmy her bottom and legs through the space she'd made. But first, she needed to get Bryan away from her.

She was just about to kick out one leg in an effort to trip him when the boat lurched again and Bryan went reeling backwards, arms pinwheeling.

"Damn it!" he howled as he crashed against the wall.

Adrenaline shot through her and her heart pounded so loudly she could feel it in her ears. If she was going to get away, the time was now. She shimmied and twisted wildly until she was able to get her hands over her feet and out from under her. Her wrists were still bound, but at least she felt a little less exposed. Bryan was still trying to find his footing on the rocking sea vessel as she pushed herself unsteadily to stand.

"Don't get cute, Stephanie," he warned as he gripped the wall and straightened, leveling the gun at her. "I don't want to shoot you, but I will."

She flicked a glance to the hatch leading out to the deck of the boat and then back at Bryan.

She would not go quietly. If they did find her body by some miracle, there would be proof of what had happened this night.

She let out a bellow and lowered her head, charging at Bryan's center mass with everything she had, sending them both crashing through the door and out onto the rain-pelted deck. Dimly, she heard the sound of gunfire. Felt a strange pressure in her thigh. Smelled the acrid scent of gunpowder.

But it was the oh-so-satisfying crack of bone that stuck with her. Apparently, skulls were stronger than ribs.

She didn't waste time celebrating the tiny victory, instead using her teeth and nails to scratch, bite, and claw. He howled in fury and sent a fist directly into her jaw. For a moment, she saw stars as nausea rolled in her belly. Her vision blurred as she tried to retain consciousness, but it was the cold whip of the stormy wind and the chill of the raindrops on her cheeks that brought her back to reality. Bryan had a death grip around her neck and was dragging her across the deck.

She fought as hard as she could, scrambling against the slippery deck as he pulled her closer to the edge where the roiling black waves awaited.

"Goodbye, Stephanie," Bryan growled a moment before he hurled her off the side.

She hit the sea hard, and the chill of it stole her breath as a massive whitecap smashed against her face, filling her mouth with briny water, dragging her under.

She kicked her feet, frantic to get to the surface. To sweet, fresh air. To her children and her sisters. To hope and a future. To justice.

Her face broke the surface for an instant before being swallowed again as she kicked and flailed.

Was this how it all ended?

Please, Paul, if you're watching over me right now, give me the strength to stay afloat just a little longer...

Chapter Twenty-Five

Anna was usually calm during a crisis, but her sister was out in the rough sea with that maniac and they were standing around twiddling their thumbs while they waited for Gabe. There had to be a faster way to get to Stephanie.

She ran up the pier toward the road and intercepted Ethan as he was coming to meet them.

"Bryan took Stephanie out to sea," she said, out of breath from her anxiety. "We have to get out there!"

Ethan's eyes flew wide with panic. "What?" But the word seemed like more of a reaction than a question. He scrubbed his hand over his face, then pinned a sharp gaze on her. "How can you be sure?"

"His boat is gone."

"Do you know the name of the boat?" Ethan asked.

"The Molly Marie," Todd said from behind Anna. "And Gabe is forty-five minutes away."

"My nephew," Anna explained. "He has a boat."

Ethan nodded with a grim look. "Stay here. I'll be right back." Then he pulled his cell phone out of his pocket and placed a call while sprinting toward the road. Anna could hear snippets of words and phrases, like he was explaining the situation to someone.

"I'm not standing around waiting," Todd said. "A friend of mine from high school lives a block away and he has a boat too. I'm running over there to get his keys." He took off before Anna could respond.

Ethan passed Todd on his way back, now wearing a rain slicker as he hurried down the dock.

"I've called the Coast Guard," he said as he approached Anna. "But I'm going out there on my own boat."

"I'm going with you!" Anna said as he pushed past her.

"It's not safe in this weather," he said, not bothering to even look over his shoulder. "You wait here."

"That's a bunch of malarkey," Anna called after him, then followed in his wake. "I'm coming."

"Coming where?" Cee-cee asked, realizing that some sort of plan had been created without her.

"Ethan has a boat," Anna said in a tone that brooked no argument. "And we're going with him."

Ethan stopped next to a boat that was smaller than a lot of the boats tied to the dock, but it looked sturdy enough to brave the rough ocean waves.

"It's going to be dangerous," he said as he started to untie the boat from its mooring.

Anna began unfastening the opposite rope. "I've looked danger in the eye and laughed in its face."

"It's true," Max said. "She has."

Ethan tossed his rope onto the boat and gave the three women an appraising glance.

"We're scrappier than we look," Anna said, lifting her chin.

"I'll probably regret this," Ethan groaned, "but climb aboard."

The women didn't waste any time getting on the boat while Ethan inserted a key into the ignition switch. The engines sprang to life, and Anna realized that the boat might not be the largest one at the dock, but it had good, strong engines that could get them out to sea faster.

Ethan pointed to a bench while he backed the boat out of its slip. "Life jackets. Wear them."

Anna quickly grabbed the life jackets and handed them out to Cee-cee and Max, then Ethan and herself, then shoved her sister and niece into the small cabin space. The rain was coming down and the waves were choppy. No sense in all of them being out in the elements and risk getting tossed overboard by the wind and the waves.

"How do you know where to go?" she asked after she got her jacket securely fastened. She was hanging on to a bar near Ethan and the steering wheel.

"I checked on the size of Perkins' boat, and it's not much larger than mine," Ethan shouted over the weather. "It's the way I would go if I had to brave these elements. I'm counting on him wanting to survive this expedition."

Anna nodded, then tried to swallow the lump in her throat. Bryan would make sure *he* survived the expedition, but he would make sure that Steph didn't. He could simply toss her out of the boat and be done with it. He didn't need to go to a certain location. He could do it anywhere.

Ethan shot Anna a determined look. "We'll find her."

She hoped he was right.

They sped along, the boat's radio crackling from time to time with chatter from the Coast Guard. About ten minutes in, a voice on the radio announced that they'd detected a blip two miles southeast of Miller Point and that the nearest Coast Guard boat was ten minutes away.

Ethan gripped the steering wheel tighter. "That's where I was heading. We're five minutes away."

"Thank God," Anna mumbled, hoping they'd reach her in time.

The rain let up, but the drizzle pelted Anna's skin as they raced across the sea, the boat pitching and bumping even more than before. Anna scanned the horizon for any sign of them. Several minutes later, she pointed her finger ahead and shouted, "I see lights. It looks like a boat. That has to be them!"

Ethan seemed more determined than before, leaning into the steering wheel as though his willpower and determination could make them go faster. "I have binoculars in that compartment," he shouted, pointing to a hatch on the helm. "Get them out and see if you can see anyone."

Anna obeyed and tried to study the boat, which proved to be difficult with the movement. The boat appeared to be stationary, and through the cabin window, she could see the silhouette of a figure that looked like it might be a man. No one else.

"The boat's not moving, no sign of her," she said, her heart plummeting to her feet. "What if he threw her overboard already?"

"Get out another life jacket," Ethan said.

He was thinking worst-case scenario too, which made her stomach cramp. She couldn't lose her sister. Not like this.

She grabbed a life jacket and a ring buoy, prepared to dive into the ocean if necessary to save Steph, then returned to her post with her binoculars.

A man burst backward through the cabin door onto the deck, another figure ramming her head into his chest. Anna was sure she recognized the gray coat with black trim.

217

"I see him!" Anna called out and Cee-cee and Max emerged from the cabin. "And I think I see Steph! She's ramming him with her head!"

Cee-cee and Max ran out onto the deck.

"Did we find her?" her sister asked.

Anna didn't answer, too intent on watching the flurry of activity on the deck of Bryan's boat. Steph seemed to be attacking him with everything she had. But Bryan was bigger and apparently stronger. He hooked an arm around her neck and began dragging her toward the back of the boat.

Anna began to panic. "Hurry, Ethan! He's about to throw her overboard!"

Stephanie resisted, making Bryan fight for purchase on the deck. The boat hit a wave, and the pair lurched, then Stephanie went over the side into the angry waves.

"He threw her over!" Anna shouted. "She's in the water!"

"Which side?" he asked.

"Port!"

They were close enough that she tossed the binoculars onto the deck.

Max reached for the wheel. "I can steer! You take care of Aunt Stephanie!"

Ethan relinquished his spot and took the life preserver from Anna, practically leaning over the side as though he thought he could swim to her faster than the boat could get them there.

Bryan glanced up and saw their boat approaching, then ran to the wheel.

"Don't you dare let him get away!" Anna said, snatching the preserver. "Cee-cee and I will save our sister. You go after that dunderhead!"

Ethan's face was so hard that Anna would have been terrified if she hadn't known he was on their side.

"Kill the engine!" Ethan shouted at Max.

She pulled back on the throttle, and the boat's momentum significantly slowed, pitching them forward.

Ethan took a running leap onto the bow of the boat as Max swung the vessel around the starboard side, avoiding Steph who was flailing in the water.

Anna tossed the ring out to her sister as Ethan jumped onto Bryan's boat, tackling the man as he tried to restart the boat's engine.

"Stephanie!" Cee-cee cried out as Steph's head went under and she didn't reemerge.

"Mom!" Max shouted, shutting the engine off and scrambling to the side of the boat. As they closed onto Bryan's boat, she grabbed one of the mooring ropes and readied herself to board. The moment Ethan's boat reached Bryan's, Max leapt on board, clutching tight to the mooring rope, as the two men continued wrestling on the deck.

Anna ran to the back of the boat, pulling the ring back in, then tossing it out again when Steph surfaced. "Grab the ring, Stephanie!"

Max tied the rope to a cleat on Bryan's boat while the men still grappled for control. She got the two vessels tethered, but the forward momentum of Ethan's boat was dragging them further away from Stephanie.

Max climbed onto the edge of Bryan's boat and hopped back in, restarting the engine and putting it into reverse.

Steph went under again and took several long seconds to reemerge, and Anna was close to hyperventilating.

Ethan now seemed to have the upper hand in their struggle and threw several punches at Bryan's face. Bryan crumpled to the deck.

"Ethan!" Anna shouted. "Stephanie!"

Ethan ran to the side of the boat, searching the water, then dove in headfirst. When he surfaced, Anna tossed the ring out toward him. Looping an arm around it, he dragged it along him as he swam toward her. He was fighting the current so hard it looked like he was swimming in slow motion, but seconds later he reached her as she went under again. Letting go of the ring, he dove again, both of them disappearing under the roiling waves.

Seconds passed and neither resurfaced.

"Stephanie!" Cee-cee wailed, leaning over the back of the boat.

Stephanie's head bobbed above the water first, Ethan right behind.

The ring was banging into the side of Bryan's boat. Anna tugged it back in, then tossed it out next to Ethan's head.

He latched on to her preserver and Anna started to tug them in just as a gunshot rang out.

Bryan had come to and was now shooting at Stephanie and Ethan in the water.

A fury rose up in Anna like Anna had never known, and she grabbed the first thing she could get her hands on— the binoculars, which had slid across the deck and were now at her feet—and threw them at Bryan as hard as she could.

They hit him in the temple, dazing him for a second, and then he shook his head.

Even angrier, Anna plucked an oar from the brackets on the side of the boat wall, and jumped onto Bryan's boat.

Bryan had moved back to the side and was blinking hard at the falling rain as he pointed his gun toward the water.

Anna snuck up behind him as the gun went off again. Raising the oar over her head, she brought it down hard, beaning him on the back of the head.

"You leave my sister alone, you chicken turd!"

Bryan sank like a rock, but she wasn't taking any chances. She snagged one of the ropes attached to a cleat on his boat and tied up his hands.

Cee-cee and Max were dragging the preserver with Ethan and Steph to the boat, but Steph was like a limp noodle in his arms.

"Stephanie?" Cee-cee called out as they reached the ladder.

Ethan started to climb up, tugging Stephanie behind him, but he was shaking so hard he couldn't get her up.

Max jumped in—Cee-cee crying in protest—and got behind her aunt, pushing on her butt to help get her into the boat.

Ethan and Steph fell to the deck with a thud, but Steph lay perfectly still.

Max climbed into the boat behind them, then felt for Stephanie's pulse. Panic filled her eyes, but she didn't hesitate as she straightened Stephanie's back and tilted her head, then began to give her mouth-to-mouth resuscitation.

Anna watched in horror, needing to do something, but she had no idea what.

Steph began to cough, and Ethan reached over and tilted her on her side as she coughed out what had to be half the ocean.

A boat with floodlights approached and a man on a loudspeaker called out, "U.S. Coast Guard. Put your hands up and prepare to board."

Ethan stood and lifted his hands as the Coast Guard vessel pulled up to the side. Then he explained the situation as they climbed onto the boat.

"Ethan!" Cee-cee called out in a panic. "Stephanie's been shot!"

Anna scanned her sister for evidence, finding a growing bloodstain on her leg.

The Coast Guard took over, rushing them all aboard and racing to Decatur, the closest town with a trauma center.

Anna, Cee-cee, and Max followed an unconscious Stephanie through the ER doors, but the hospital staff kicked them out and told them to go to the waiting room.

Ethan found them there, his face tight with worry.

"Any word?"

Anna shook her head, fighting the urge to cry. "No. Nothing. They won't let us back with her."

His jaw set and he marched through the emergency room doors, holding up his badge. "I'm Detective Jenkins with the Bluebird Bay Police, and I am going back to see Stephanie Ketterman."

Then he ignored the nurses' shouts of protest and marched down the hall.

Ten minutes later, he came back into the waiting room, a nurse following behind, chewing him out like a clucking hen.

Anna and Cee-cee jumped to their feet.

"Well?" Anna demanded. "Spit it out, man. How is she?"

A relieved grin cracked his serious expression. "She needs surgery to remove the bullet in her leg, and they'll want to keep her for a few days to watch her, but they expect a full recovery."

Anna sagged with relief and Max snagged an arm around her back to support her.

"I swear to all that is holy, if Stephanie ever scares me like that again...," Anna said.

"If that's not calling the kettle black," Cee-cee muttered.

Anna shrugged with a grin. "Then let's just say the Sullivan girls' days of adventure are done."

"Hey," Max protested with an ornery look. "As a Sullivan girl by default, I say my days of adventure are just beginning."

Cee-cee pressed a hand to her chest. "Heaven help us all."

Anna just smiled at her niece. This felt a lot like passing her torch on to the next generation, and she wouldn't have it any other way.

Epilogue

F *our months later...*

The air was balmy and the skies were clear and blue. It was the perfect day for a wedding. Tears rushed to Stephanie's eyes as she imagined her beautiful daughter walking down the aisle later that evening. They'd be surrounded by supportive, loving family and friends. Todd would be giving Sarah away, which would be bittersweet. In fact, as Stephanie contemplated the coming hours, it would've been easy to turn melancholy. To lament all the important milestones Paul would miss out on, and what her children would achieve and experience in their lives without their father around to cheer them on or to comfort them when they needed it. Instead, she remembered what Dr. Yang had told her: Focus on the times they did have together. On being grateful for the love and the experiences they'd shared. And they'd shared a lifetime of those.

Jeff's first steps and his first fall. Sarah's spelling bee win and her crushing defeat as champ the following year. All the wounded animals Todd had nursed back to health...and the ones he hadn't been able to save.

Life was a carousel. A beautiful, dizzying ride of ups and downs, and she'd been beyond blessed to share decades on that ride with Paul.

Warm, strong fingers clasped hers, and she looked up to find Ethan smiling down at her encouragingly.

"Ready?"

She looked out at the water one last time and sent a final, silent prayer of thanks and love to her beloved husband, and then she turned.

"As ready as I'm going to get."

Cee-cee, Max, and Anna had all hung back to give her some time alone, but now they padded through the sand toward her. Max turned and called over her shoulder.

"We're ready!"

Todd, who was standing in the parking lot a hundred feet away, shielded his eyes from the midmorning sun and gave her the okay sign before turning toward Mick and Beckett, who stood behind his flatbed waiting.

"Ready!"

Ethan released Stephanie's hand. "Be right back."

Her sisters and her niece drifted closer as they watched the men maneuver Shelley the turtle out of the back of the truck on a gurney.

"Is it seriously possible he's grown?" Anna marveled, shaking her head in awe as the men slid the turtle off the gurney and onto a makeshift sled Mick had made out of plexiglass.

"Maybe he got into something radioactive and we're looking at the next Godzilla," Cee-cee quipped.

Stephanie had to agree with her sisters, Shelley looked massive in the bright light of day, but that was a good thing. When he'd come to her, he'd been near death. Shell shattered, deeply wounded, almost beyond repair. Now here he was, hale, hearty, and best of all, whole again. Granted, it had taken months of healing, more than a pint of shellac, and countless sticks, but she couldn't be more proud of how robust he looked. Shelley had the entire ocean before him, and the possibilities were endless.

A lot had changed in the past year, Stephanie realized with a start. For both her turtle friend and for herself. She'd never thought she would be able to find joy again, never mind love. But then, there it was. What she felt for Ethan was different than what she'd felt for Paul, but it was just as real. Just as true. And they were only getting started.

Not that their beginnings had been exactly smooth sailing. She'd been so focused on the past, she'd nearly missed the future that was right in front of her. As the men pulled Shelley across the sugary sand, Stephanie's thoughts drifted to Bryan.

He'd been the one to take Paul's phone, and confessed to destroying it soon after Paul's murder. If he'd never come into her clinic, would she have gone the rest of her life without knowing he was responsible for Paul's death? Or would he have heard about her poking around in Paul's affairs and have succeeded in killing her as well? She'd never know because he was spending the next twenty years behind bars after accepting a plea bargain for felony murder, kidnapping, and attempted murder that had taken premeditated murder along with a mandatory life sentence off the table. He'd be an old man before he managed to get out, and she certainly wouldn't be going to visit him to ask any more questions. She'd finally gotten the truth she'd so desperately needed, and now she knew:

Her husband had loved her as fiercely as she'd loved him. He'd been exactly the man she'd always believed him to be, and then some. He'd risked his very life to make sure justice was served, and by some amazing stroke of luck she still hadn't quite been able to process, she'd managed to complete that task for him. She'd finally done it. She'd finally found what she'd been looking for all these years, both for her beloved husband, and for herself.

Peace.

She swallowed past the lump in her throat and nodded, getting weepy again as they all moved closer to the shoreline, where the waves lapped at the sand, with Shelley in tow.

"We're going to miss you, big guy," Anna murmured, her eyes going suspiciously glassy as she reached down and patted the turtle's leathery head.

"You are a prince among turtles," Max added, stroking his extra-shiny shell, her lips tilted in a bittersweet smile.

Stephanie watched as each of them said goodbye to their friend Shelley. When they'd finished, she knelt beside him.

"It's been an honor," she murmured, her gaze tripping over his stitched shell, looking for a sign of fissures or cracks one last time. There were none. Shelley was truly ready to head back out into his natural habitat again, and it was up to her to send him on his way. She grinned as he suddenly seemed to catch the scent and sight of the water and his feet began to move, sliding against the plexiglass.

By tacit agreement, they all gathered around and began tugging the makeshift sled to where the sea and the sand met. The second the water sluiced and roiled around Shelley's feet, the animal's joy was almost palpable. He slipped along the plexiglass as he tried to launch himself forward. It took a couple of tries and a lot of squeaking and sliding, but then he was in motion, cutting gracefully through the shallow water.

227

Tears coursed down Stephanie's face now, unchecked, as she watched him. What if a shark got him? Or if he got tangled in a fishing net?

But she shut those fearful thoughts away before they could take root. Shelley was big and strong and would likely live a long, happy life. She'd done everything she could to ensure that. The rest was out of her hands.

There would always be a little of that now, she suspected. The fear. That was how it went when tragedy struck, taking something from a person when they least expected. But that wouldn't stop her from living or loving or taking risks. Not anymore.

This time around, she'd have to make sure to appreciate every moment just a little more. Every breath. Soak in the moments, both big and small, and hold them close to her heart.

And as Ethan slipped his arm around her shoulder to pull her close, and Todd moved to her side to take her hand even as her sisters and niece flanked her, she took a snapshot of it all in her mind so she would never forget how many times she'd been blessed.

She blew out a sigh and nodded to herself. It was time to go. She had a gorgeous royal blue chiffon dress to slip into and her amazing daughter's wedding to attend. Stephanie spared one last glance at the ocean as Shelley disappeared from sight.

Goodbye, my turtle friend.
Goodbye, Paul, my love.
See you both on the other side.

About the Author

Denise Grover Swank was born in Kansas City, Missouri and lived in the area until she was nineteen. Then she became nomadic, living in five cities, four states and ten houses over the course of ten years before she moved back to her roots. She speaks English and smattering of Spanish and Chinese which she learned through an intensive Nick Jr. immersion period. Her hobbies include witty Facebook comments (in own her mind) and dancing in her kitchen with her children. (Quite badly if you believe her offspring.) Hidden talents include the gift of justification and the ability to drink massive amounts of caffeine and still fall asleep within two minutes. Her lack of the sense of smell allows her to perform many unspeakable tasks. She has six children and hasn't lost her sanity. Or so she leads you to believe.

For more info go to: dgswank.com or denisegroverswank.com

About the Author

Christine Gael is the women's fiction writing alter-ego of USA Today Bestselling contemporary romance author, Christine Bell, and NYT Bestselling paranormal romance author, Chloe Cole.

Christine lives with her sweet, funny husband in South Florida, where she spends the majority of her day writing and consuming mass amounts of coffee. Her favorite pastimes include playing pickle ball and tennis year-round, and texting pictures of palm trees and the beach to her New England-based friends in the wintertime.

While Christine enjoys all types of writing but, at age 46, she's especially excited to be creating stories that will hopefully both entertain and empower the women in her own age group.

For more information visit her website at christinegael.com

Now available from Christine Gael
Maeve's Girls

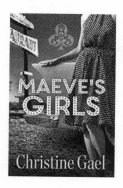

If you're reading this, that means I've gone to the big casino in the sky...

Thibodaux, Louisiana had never seen anything like Maeve Blanchard, and they never will again. After 75 years, five husbands, four daughters, and one bootleg whiskey ring, Maeve has finally been called home to be with the Lord...or with someone, somewhere, at any rate.

But while Maeve took her impending demise in stride and dove into death with the same gusto as she did life, her four girls have had their worlds turned upside down.

Fifty-four-year-old Lena, Maeve's love-child, left home at sixteen to get away from the stain of her mother's wild life and never looked back. Kate, who married far too young, lost herself somewhere along the way. Sasha, who has followed in her mother's high-heeled footsteps, is forced to come face to face with her own mortality. Maggie, Maeve's niece who she raised as her own, always wondered where she fit in.

Maeve's girls will need to work through their grief over the loss of their complicated mother, and they're ready to come home to Thibodaux to do it. But, is Thibodaux is ready for them?